They Call Me Law 3
When a Good Girl Meets a Thug

By Kelly Marie

Chapter One
Honey

Three days later

My ass was still hiding from Ky-mani. Tasha
told me he went to my old job the next morning
looking for me and she told him about me being fired.
He went ballistic and was demanding that she told
him where I was but she said she didn't know.

My phone was still off, but I cut it on quickly
just to disable my 'find my iPhone' setting so he
couldn't track my ass down. But I wished I hadn't.
Monae had sent me a few more pics of her and Ky-
mani. One with his hand pushing her head down
further on his dick. I felt sick!

I also had a few messages and missed calls from
his family. I felt bad for them because I knew they
would have been looking for me and worried. I sent

3

Nevaeh a quick message to let her know I was ok and to tell Marco that I would see him soon once I got myself together.

As soon as I sent the text, Ky-mani's name flashed on my screen as he called me.

In my panic, I answered it. "Honey, baby please!" I heard him say before I disconnected the call and turned my phone off. *Shit.* I thought shaking my head.

I told Ky-mani, in the beginning, I'm not a female who took disrespect. His ass should have never been over there in the first place. He told me he was with the boys. He would have never gone over there without telling me unless he was on some bullshit, which he was.

All of this drama was just too much for me. Monae's ass, Angel's ass, my job, my apartment, my father, those niggas, all of it, I was sick! It was time I looked out for me and made myself happy. Before Ky-mani and fighting bitches over dick, my girls and I had the best times together. So, what better way to get back to me than my girls?

I used my iPad to FaceTime Tasha.

4

"What up, my bitch?" she smiled at me.

This bitch was eating…no fucking surprise there. "What up greedy bitch," I laughed.

"How are you holding up?"

"As good as I can be."

"You know Ky-mani out here tearing this town up looking for your ass?"

"Oh well," I shrugged my shoulders and she laughed.

"I'm dead ass serious. Bitch he found all our addresses and he keeps driving past looking for you," she said and we both screamed laughing.

"Nigga is going off his head for real," she laughed, wiping tears away.

"I swear, I woke up one morning about to leave out for work and his ass was sitting outside in his car," she laughed.

"Talking about, morning Tasha I was in the area. Nigga, how you know it was my area?" she said and I held my stomach laughing.

"Bitch, you dropped that good pussy on him, got him going loco out this bitch. Don't be surprised when he eventually tracks that ass down. His dick gonna track that pussy down like a bloodhound," she said and I laughed my ass off.

5

This is why I loved my bitches, it was nothing but love and jokes all day every damn day.

"I was thinking that maybe we could go to Club Trinity on Saturday?" I asked and this bitch started dancing.

"Oh yeah, that's what I'm talking about. You know me and the girls are gonna have to be on some separate 007 shit to get to you? With Ky-mani's ass camping outside our houses," she laughed.

"Shit, I wouldn't be surprised if his ass was out there right now with some listening devices." We both laughed.

"Thank you, Tasha. I know it's not been easy with Ky-mani on your ass."

"Girl, please. At least I know you would do the same for me when I need to hide from Chase's black ass."

"Bitch, please we all know it will be Chase's ass that we'll be hiding from your crazy ass," I laughed and she laughed too.

"You ain't never lied," she laughed.

"Alrighty Saturday and be safe, Honey. Love you," she said.

"Love you too," I said and we waved bye to

each other.

I couldn't lie I did feel something knowing he was going crazy looking for me but oh well.

***

Two days later

It was finally Saturday and I sat dressed ready to party waiting for my girls to arrive. I felt bad because they had to do all kinds of movements just to meet me. They went a hundred locations before making their way to me. Ky-mani and his boys were on their ass it was no joke. But luckily they slipped through and got away.

When I heard knocking on my door, I got up and ran to the door. I pulled it open and they literally jumped on my ass. It had been five days since I saw them and that was five days too long.

"Bitch, if you ever saw what we had to do just to get here," Kelis said.

"Don't be surprised if you don't hear from us for a while because I just know them niggas gone fuck us up on sight," Sydney said laughing.

"Why, what y'all do?" I asked, taking a seat.

"Bitch, Ky-mani followed my ass all the way to Kelis' asking me if I wanted him to drop me off. And Ricky followed Sydney. So, we get to Kelis' and all three of them are there talking about they know we know where you at. So, of course, we acted dumb. So Ky-mani leaves says he going somewhere but leaves the other two to watch us," Tasha starts and my ass is glued to her every word.

"So we decided we gon' go on out. Ricky and Drake follow us. Bitch, we just drove for the hell of it. We took their asses all over the goddamn town. So, Sydney comes up with a plan to lose them. She tells us to pull up at the gas station. She gets out and starts chatting to Ricky as Drake follows Kelis in the store. My ass climbs out of the car, crawls along the floor and lets the air out their tires."

"As soon as those suckers were all flat, we took off running to Kelis' car. I saw Drake grab his phone, so I knew his ass was calling Ky-mani. Bitch, we drove out of there like we just stole from a bank," Tasha said and we all laughed hard.

My girls were some gangsta bitches for real. I

can't believe them niggas were following them like that. But good serves them right.

We laughed and laughed our asses off. We weren't shit. I knew Ky-mani was gon' fuck their asses up but for now, it was party time.

"Oh, bitch, if Ky-mani ever caught your ass in that, he would beat your ass," Tasha said, looking at me and shaking her head.

I had on a black, strapless jumpsuit that had a love heart shaped top and nude peep toe red bottoms. I straightened my hair with a middle part and put a little blush on my face with highlighter and did a smoky eye look. My lips had a mauve lipstick and chestnut lip liner from MAC.

"What?" I asked her because I didn't see anything wrong with what I had on. It wasn't tight or short.

"Bitch, I'm looking at you and all I can see is your cleavage and your ass and hips in that jumpsuit. Sexy, bitch," she said and we all laughed.

"Let's go," I said, shaking my head and opening the door.

We jumped in my car and headed for Club Trinity that was in the next town.

The streets were pumping and were lit! The club was pumping some beats and me and my girls were looking fly. We grabbed some bar stools and started to party. I was moving my hips and bobbing to the beats. Jhene Aiko was blasting in the club and there wasn't a person sitting in the room.

Some nigga next to me tried dropping some lyrics on me but I curved his ass.

I got the bar tender's attention and ordered four glasses of Hpnotiq. My girls and I toasted and sipped on our drinks.

An hour into it and my girls and I were nice, not drunk, just nice.

Kelis and Tasha started having a dance off and Sydney and I laughed at their stupid asses.

"Who won? Me innit?" Tasha said and we laughed at them.

"Bitch, I won!" Kelis countered.

"Nah, bitch, I did. I got a little more ass than you. Not my fault Chase keeps slapping up my batty," she said and we all laughed.

"Ladies, you're both earth's dumbest hoes, so

you both win," I said and Sydney slapped me a high five.

"Thanks," Tasha said and smiled.

Only a damn fool would thank being called dumb and a hoe!

She grabbed the rest of her drink and finished it. She dropped it on the bar and turned to say something to me with her back against the bar but stopped.

"Oh shit," she said, staring behind me.

"What?" I said, looking at her.

"Ky-mani is here and he's watching your ass," she said and I popped my eyes open.

"Shut the fuck up," I said and she nodded.

I slowly turned around and there he was. Sitting up in the V.I.P section, staring at me.

"Shit!" I spat and turned around again. "Shit," I said again.

"What's going on?" Sydney asked so I told her that he was there.

"We gotta get out of here," Kelis said and I nodded. I discreetly picked up my clutch and made sure my keys were on the top.

"Bitch, if we gonna move it has to be now because his ass just got up," Tasha said tapping my hand.

"Go!" I yelled and the four of us took off running.

We pushed past the crowd and security and ran for our lives.

"Bitch, he coming!" Tasha screamed and I ran faster.

"Oh shit, he gone catch my ass," Tasha said, slowing down.

I looked back and he was gaining on us with Ricky and Drake right behind him.

"Bitch, your ass better run like they about to give out the last fucking piece of fried chicken," I yelled at her.

This bitch took off like she was fucking Usain Bolt and reached my car first. I pressed the button unlocking the car and we jumped in.

"Honey!" I heard him scream after me. I managed to start the car and hit the peddle just as he caught up to my car and grabbed the door handle.

I tore out of that parking lot tires screeching and shit.

"Yo, how the fuck did he find us?" I said, out of breath and checking my mirror.

"I don't know," Tasha said behind me.

"Do you think he knows where you staying at?" Sydney asked and I shook my head.

"If he knew he would have waited there for me, he wouldn't have gone to the club," I said and hoped.

"Oh, shit," Tasha said.

"What!" I panicked, looking behind me.

"He saw my Facebook status," she said and I looked at her from my mirror.

"What Facebook status, Tasha?" I asked.

"The one where I said going to Club Trinity with my home girls. And I tagged your ass," she said in a child's voice. "And he liked my status," she said.

Fuck it, it was done.

We all busted out laughing. This nigga spoke about not being on Facebook like that but his ass liked Tasha's status. He was a determined nigga I ain't even gone lie. And he looked fine ass fuck. With his dreads loose, a white tee on, blue jeans, and white Timberlands on his feet. He looked like he was more ripped since I last saw him. Seeing his face made my pussy jump.

It was a shame how things ended up but he hurt me and after everything I went through with Jerome, I didn't expect Ky-mani to do that to me.

I tore through the streets and got to my hotel quick time. We couldn't even stop to talk, my girls had to go. They jumped in Kelis' car and raced off. I quickly took my ass inside.

I took a bath and walked around the suite waiting to hear from my girls. It had been an hour, so they should have been back by now.

I jumped when my FaceTime on my iPad started ringing. I answered but stood out of range.

"Bitch, where you at?!" I heard Tasha's voice.

"Shit, I thought it was him. What happened? Did he catch y'all?" I said.

"Bitch, his ass was sitting right outside Kelis' when we got back. He even called Chase on my ass," we screeched laughing so hard.

"Hoe, stop lying."

"I swear; his ass was out there too. Ky-mani was snitching on us hard to Chase," she continued to laugh.

"So what happened?"

"Well after Ky-mani tore us a new ass. Our niggas yoked our asses up. But it wasn't all bad because Chase gave me that angry sex and you know how I like that shit," she smiled widely and I shook my head.

"So Chase wasn't mad?" I asked.

"Nah. He said he understands that I'm protecting my girl and how you come first, etc. You know how he is about you, girl," she said and I nodded.

"Well, bitch, thanks for a fun filled night but my ass tired from all that fucking running and dodging their asses. Sleep well and hit me up tomorrow," she smiled and waved.

I blew a kiss to her and ended the call.

When I climbed in the bed, I couldn't help but laugh. This nigga really chased me around town.

He must be really desperate. I laughed myself to sleep.

Chapter Two
Law

A nigga like me was going crazy without my baby. She had been missing for days and it was killing me. I looked every fucking where for her but still I couldn't find her.

I knew she wasn't in Texas because all her I.D was destroyed in the fire so she couldn't travel. Which was good for me because I damn sure didn't want to call Momma P and explain that I had no idea where her daughter was.

I was so angry that I kept turning up at Monae's house and cussing her ass out.

I was sick without my woman. I couldn't even sleep.

My momma tried everything to help me through it, to comfort me and get me to eat but I couldn't. A big part of me was missing.

I almost burned that fucking building down when I turned up at Honey's job only to be told they fired her! Like when the fuck did that shit happen?

Tasha explained what happened the same day Monae posted shit about me. So, when my baby was at home crying about her job, I was getting my dick posted all over Facebook by Monae. No wonder she took off. She needed me and instead, that's what she got.

I knew her girls knew where she was but they were protecting her. I could see in their faces that they didn't really want to talk to me.

Like I said they were a different kind. Any other bitches would have loved the fact they thought I fucked up and would be lining up for the dick but not these females.

Their loyalty was to Honey and I couldn't hate them for that.

I wasn't shit, though. I got their addresses from my friends at the police precinct. They didn't have to tell me where Honey was, I would just let them lead me to her.

I drove up and down past their houses but I never saw any trace of Honey.

My niggas were on it too, maybe because they now knew that Honey was their sister! They were on the girls' asses twenty-four sevens.

We followed their asses to work, the store, every fucking where and sooner or later their asses were going to slip up and lead me to Honey.

I stationed Ricky outside Sydney's block, KY at Tasha's, and Drake at Kelis' if their asses moved I would know. I wasn't playing with them.

It was my day to collect the kids from school. I was so fucked up in the head over Honey that I couldn't even laugh and joke with the kids like I used to.

"Daddy, where is Honey? Why can't we go see her?" Chyna asked.

"Um, baby Honey is not around at the moment. She's mad at Daddy," I said.

"Is she mad at me too for lying, Daddy?" She said. I looked up in the mirror and I saw her crying. I pulled over the car and turned to face her.

"Na Na, why you crying, baby? And what do you mean by you lied?" I asked, stroking her cheeks.

"Mommy told me to call you and tell you that I was having nightmares and couldn't sleep. She beat

18

me when I said no because you and Honey told me lying is bad. But Mommy said if I did it wasn't lying because Mommy said. So, I called you Daddy and you came," she cried hard.

"Is that why Honey is gone? Is it because I lied and got you in trouble with her? I heard Momma saying she was gone," Chyna said.

I ain't gonna lie, I was beyond angry!

"Chyna, you listen to Daddy lying is bad even if an adult tells you to, you should never lie ok?" I said and she nodded.

"And Honey is not mad at you I promise. Daddy will get her back soon," I said wiping her tears away.

I turned around and drove off again. This trifling ass bitch was the worse! When I arrived at Monae's, I brought the kids in and put them up in their room with a snack and movie. I made sure they were set before I went down to their hoe ass momma.

She was sitting on the couch reading a magazine. I walked right up to her and grabbed by the throat.

I dragged her to the wall and slammed her body into it hard. She winced out in pain.

19

"Bitch, if you ever whoop my daughter again, I will fucking murder your stank ass! Don't put your fucking hands on my daughter behind your bullshit. Making her ass call me and lie about having nightmares just so you could lure me here," I said and her eyes grew wide.

"You better pray to God that I find Honey by next week or I'm coming back for your ass and you won't like me, Monae, I promise you that. And don't even think about pulling Chyna up about telling me. I dare you to fuck with me, Monae. Honey already left my ass, so I have nothing else to lose behind fucking your ass up," I snarled in her face. I stood and held her for a few more seconds to let my words marinate.

I walked out of that bitch slamming the door behind me. I climbed into my car and punched the steering wheel.

I took off and headed to Tasha's to sit out there with KY since he didn't have a car. When I got there, he was sitting on the sidewalk directly opposite her house. When I pulled up, he jumped in the passenger seat.

"What up, Law?" he said, dapping me up.

"All good. So, anything?" I asked and he

shook his head.

"No sign of Honey but Tasha keeps looking out the window at my ass. I think she about to step out," he said.

I fired up a blunt and fixed my eyes on her house. Sure enough, she came out of the house. She looked up at us and I smiled at her. KY laughed when she didn't smile back. Ignoring us, she took off and started walking.

I offered her a ride to wherever she was going but she declined. KY and I laughed our asses off as we followed her all the way to Kelis' house. When we pulled up, Ricky was outside too after following Sydney's ass.

We all climbed out of our cars and approached the door. The ladies opened the door before we could even knock on the door.

"Evening, ladies," I smiled at them.

"Honey isn't here, Ky-mani," Kelis said, folding her arms.

"I know but if she comes, I'll be here to catch her and if y'all go to her, I will still catch her," I smiled and they shook their heads at me.

"Ky-mani, for real we are not seeing Honey

today. We are just having our girls' night in," Tasha said.

"Hmmm mmmm, girls' night in my ass," I said and my niggas laughed.

"It's all good, I can do this all fucking day every day," I winked before we backed up to our cars. We heard them suck their teeth before closing back the door.

"Y'all stay here, let me just grab something from the office really quick. If they move, you move and call me. I ain't playing with their asses today," I said and dapped them up.

I jumped in my car and headed to my office. I needed to load up my cash from the night before in the safe until I could get to the bank.

I wasn't even in the office an hour before Drake called me. "What's good, Drake?"

"Yo, Law, these chicks are scandalous man. They fucking let our tires down and fucked off," Drake said.

"What the fuck you mean? Where the fuck are you?" "At the gas station on Franklin," he said.

Fuck! I just knew those girls knew where her ass was, and my niggas go and lose them.

When I pulled up at the gas station all I could do was laugh. Those chicks were ruthless for real. They couldn't even let down one or two tires, they had to do all four?

They were making sure they weren't getting followed. We truly had our fucking hands full that's for certain.

When I stepped out my car, they tried to explain but I didn't even want to hear it.

"Y'all a bunch of street niggas and three chicks outsmarted you?" I said, shaking my head.

"Those motherfuckers ain't normal. They've been touched in the fucking head or something. They think of shit, that doesn't even enter into other people's minds," Drake spat and I shook my head.

I sat on my car hood and thought about what to do next. My hair was pulled back in a ponytail so I loosened that shit to help me think better.

I was hoping Monae posting what I told her to, would have made a difference but obviously not.

"Fuck me!" I roared. Fucking five days and she's still gone!

23

I don't know why but I took my phone out and found myself strolling through Facebook. I went to Honey's page and she hadn't posted anything recently, same for Kelis and Sydney. I was about to put my phone back when by accident I clicked Tasha's page.

"No fucking way," I laughed and jumped off my car. "Y'all see this," I said, handing them my phone.

"Get the fuck out. Their ass is going to Club Trinity," Drake said and I nodded.

Tasha had updated her status tagging Honey's ass. She told me exactly where they were going to be.

We quickly jumped in my car and rushed home. We needed guns and I wanted to change clothes.

I threw on a white tee, blue jeans, and white timberlands. I put my nine in my waistband and leaving my dreads loose, I was ready.

I couldn't believe her ass had the cheek to go out and party like my ass hadn't been looking for her for five fucking days! If I didn't love her so much I would have beat her ass. Once this was all over I was breaking this dick off in her ass over and over again until she learned that I was the boss.

24

We headed straight for the V.I.P section upstairs so I could scope the place out and find Honey but I didn't have to look long or hard because she was the baddest female in that bitch.

She stood out in her black jumpsuit looking extra fine. It hugged my ass that I missed so much, oh so nicely making my dick stand up. She looked so fucking beautiful it hurt that I couldn't touch her.

When Drake's "One Dance" started playing, I watched as she wined and moved her waist like a belly dancer.

My baby had my dick so hard.

"Damn," I said, grabbing my dick. Every man had their eyes on her as she moved her sexy ass to the music. I was jealous but I wasn't because it felt good knowing that every nigga in there wished she was theirs. But it was my dick that fit that pussy.

Me and my niggas thought of how we could get to her without her taking off but I never got the chance because Tasha clocked my ass. When Honey turned to look for herself I melted. My baby was motherfucking bad.

Her face lit up the dark room with her pretty ass features and bright eyes. Her breasts looked good

25

enough to eat in that outfit. My body missed her so much.

She turned back around and I saw her grab her clutch; she was going to run.

"Niggas, let's roll; she about to run." I got up and as soon as I did, her ass took off running.

"Shit!" I yelled and I rushed through the crowd downstairs after her. As I got outside, I saw her sexy, little ass running towards her car.

My car was in the front on the other side, I wouldn't get to it in time to then catch up with her car.

I had no choice but to run after her.

She didn't look it and she had heels on but my baby could run. She was fast. I held my waist so my gun wouldn't drop and ran after her ass.

She unlocked her car and climbed in with her girls.

"Honey, please!" I yelled as I got to her car. I tapped on the window and pulled on the handle but she had locked the door. She looked at me full of fear before speeding off.

"Fuck!" I yelled as I watched the car

disappear.

"Ayo, y'all niggas, need to be fucking the shit outta yo girls, man," I said. I was pissed.

First, they pretended not to know where Honey was at and then they're helping her get away.

"Come on, y'all, I ain't finished with their ass," I said, walking to my car.

First stop was to Tasha's house. I wasn't a snitch but it was time we niggas handled these women. So, I was there to see her husband.

After knocking on the door, he opened it a few seconds later.

"Hey, what's up. I'm Ky-mani, Honey's boyfriend," I said, introducing myself and he shook my hand.

"Yeah what's up. I'm Chase. Nice to meet you."

"I won't take up your time but I don't know if you know Honey has taken off after a little problem. I've been trying my hardest to find her but her girls haven't helped," I said and he shook his head.

"Damn welcome to my world. It's been my ass

against them four crazy asses for God knows how many years," he threw his hands in the air. "What they do now?" he said and I let him know about this wild goose chase tonight and the tires.

I wasn't a snitch by far but when it came to females I would tell a nigga everything so they could handle that ass.

"Let me roll out with you. That damn crazy Tasha," he said, grabbing his keys and shutting the door behind him.

He jumped in his car and followed behind me to Kelis' house. Since their night started there, I had a feeling it was going to end there and I was right. The girls looked like they were about to piss themselves when they saw me, Ricky, Drake, and Chase blocking the driveway.

"Bring your asses out the car," Chase yelled and I dapped him up. He was on the same page as me and I liked it.

"Y'all think shit is funny. Have my niggas and me following you around town. I knew y'all know where she is at. And then when I find her, y'all helping her get away from me," I said to them.

28

"Ky-mani, sorry but if it was one of your boys, you wouldn't tell us either," Tasha said.

"Yeah, I would," I lied because I wouldn't say shit.

"Oh please, if Drake went missing, you wouldn't tell me shit," Kelis said and Drake shook his head.

"We know y'all niggas have that bros before hoes code. But guess what, we have ours, chicks before dicks," Tasha said, folding her arms.

"Yeah what?!" they all said, dapping each other up.

"Tasha, bring your crazy ass here," Chase said.

But this crazy chick started dancing and we couldn't help but laugh.

"Y'all some crazy females I ain't even gone lie," I said laughing.

"But on some real shit, tell me where Honey is," I said and they shook their heads at me.

"For real, Ky-mani, we ain't going to do that," Kelis said.

"Ladies come on now, why would I fuck Monae when I had a beauty like Honey? That shit doesn't even make sense," I said with my arms out.

"That's what I was saying. If you niggas are gonna cheat, at least upgrade," Tasha laughed and I guess Chase had enough because he walked over and yoked her ass up and made her stand right next to him.

And that's why my ass snitched! He put his foot down! I knew I liked that nigga.

"I didn't cheat on Honey!" I said and they looked at me.

"What the hell I gotta lie for? Can't nobody do shit to me anyway, so why I need to lie?" I said and my niggas laughed.

I wasn't lying. Only scared niggas lied because somebody could do something if they knew the truth. But couldn't a bitch or nigga out there do anything to me!

"Ky-mani, honestly she still loves you. She was talking about how fine you look and how your dreads are down how she like. That girl ain't going nowhere but she needs time. Let her come to you Ky-mani," Kelis said but I wasn't trying to hear that shit.

"Ladies come on," I said but they shook their heads. I looked at the boys and nodded my head to let them know to handle their shit.

Immediately, they yoked up their women's ass

and took them away.

I sat in my car alone thinking. All I needed was a chance to explain to Honey but she wasn't allowing it.

All I knew was if I didn't find my baby soon, I was going to lose my ever- loving mind!

Chapter Three

Monae

The bitch was finally gone. I knew because Law made it his duty to turn up at my house and cuss me out for her being gone. He was having a major meltdown because her ass was missing when he couldn't give two fucks if he saw me or not.

Goddamn was her pussy that good?! I knew she was a pretty bitch but I also knew only pussy could make a nigga lose his mind like that.

He was even mad at Angel's ass and she didn't do shit to him.

That post was still up and he had people laugh at me in the streets. But he didn't care, all he cared about was where Honey was. I hated to admit it but I wished her ass would just come back. I couldn't take the constant cussing from him. He hated my ass even more!

I almost passed out from fear when he found out I made Chyna call his ass that night. I always knew she was a damn daddy's girl. I wanted to whoop her ass so bad but I knew she would just tell his ass. He was already at his breaking point with me; I didn't need to push him any further.

He was losing his damn mind. His family forever cussed my ass out for what he was going through. He was bugging out on them and breaking shit wherever he went. He was leaving a trail of destruction behind him like a fucking hurricane.

He even put up a Facebook post asking niggas and bitches to call him if they saw Honey.

Word around town was that he saw her but she got away from him. I know that made him worse.

He spent all day looking for her and all night. He hardly ate or slept. That was not what I wanted, I just wanted Honey gone so I could fuck my baby daddy, trick his ass into having another baby, and be with him.

That's all I wanted; what was wrong with that?

But all I managed to do was make an Incredible

Hulk version of Law and plain Law was bad enough!!!
Everywhere I went people cussed my ass out for
driving Law to that point. He was taking his frustration
out on the town and the town was blaming me.

Even my neighbors cussed my ass out; fucking
nosey, old people. How the fuck they knew Law
anyway?!

The kids weren't talking to me either. They knew
Honey was gone because something that I did. And
Chyna had an attitude because I told her to lie to her
precious daddy.

Man, I even tried to call Honey's cell and that
shit was off. She really was hiding. Not even Killa
knew where she was. He was glad I made them break
up but he was pissed that she took off somewhere and
he couldn't find her. He was so mad; he wouldn't even
give me the dick.

Why was this bitch so important that
everybody's whole existence was fucked up now that
she was gone? It just was not fair! Why couldn't I be
her?!

I hated the bitch with a passion – but Honey,

where the fuck are you?!!!

Honey

Today marked 10 days since I had been hiding from Ky-mani and five since he almost caught me at the club. He hounded my girls daily but they held out. I had not seen them since that night because it was far too risky, plus after the stunt, they pulled to get here, Ky-mani wasn't taking any chances.

But today I was going to see them because the guys had an important meeting that they couldn't miss. Ky-mani warned them not to come but we were gangsta bitches and our asses never listened!

Kelis and Sydney arrived first. We popped open some drinks and ordered room service as we waited for Tasha.

A little while later and she came knocking on the door.

36

"Hoe, it's about time your ass got here," I smiled, pulling her in. The bitches were all together so it was time to turn it the fuck up.

We sat down with our drinks and chatted until our food arrived. When a knock came, I put down my drink and went to open the door. I pulled it open expecting it to be room service but it was Chase!

"Shit! Chase," Tasha said. "What are you doing here?" she asked.
"What is your ass doing here and you two?" he threw his question at the girls. "I know damn well Ky-mani told y'all not to come by. But I told him y'all wouldn't listen," he said, shaking his head.

"How did you find us?" I asked.
"I followed Tasha after I dropped her off, talking about a job interview my ass," he said and we all turned and looked at her.
"You don't think Ky-mani told me about y'all sneaky asses?" He folded his arms.

"Tasha, didn't I tell your scary ass to learn how to drive, bitch?" I said and we started laughing.
"I don't find shit funny, sis. Why can't you just

talk to Ky-mani and see what he has to say?" Chase said but I didn't answer.

"You know you wrong to have him looking for you like that," he added and I looked down at the floor.

The door knocked again but I no longer had any appetite. Chase pulled open the door and I could have died a thousand deaths because in walked Ky-mani and he looked beyond pissed.

"Chase!" the girls shouted at him.

"What? Thugs stick together," he said, dapping Ky-mani.

The girls busted out laughing.

"Boy, you ain't no thug," Tasha laughed her ass off.

"What you say, Tasha? Don't get fucked up," he said and her ass went as quiet as a church mouse.

"That's what I thought," Chase laughed.

"Honey, really? You got me running around town going out of my mind for almost two weeks like this is a game. You know how much money I owe my momma for breaking shit in her house because of how mad I was looking for you?" he said but I couldn't even

38

answer.

"Honey, go get your stuff and let's go home," he said but I crossed my arms and didn't move.

"Honey, don't play with me. Go get your stuff now," he said a little firmer.

"Who's talking Ky-mani or Law?" I said and he smirked.

"Pick one," he said.

But I still didn't move.

"Ladies, y'all know that I wouldn't physically hurt Honey, right?" he asked and they nodded their heads.

"Good," he said before charging me and lifting me over his shoulder.

"Oh shoot. Bitch ,you shoulda ran," Tasha laughed.

"Ten. Days. Honey. This. Is. Not. A. Joke," he said, smacking my ass after each word.

"You. Don't. Listen," he continued smacking me. "Ky-mani, put me down now," I demanded.

"Or what?"

"Or I will kick your ass."

"You ain't gonna do shit," he smacked me

again.

"Come let me holler at you for a second," Ky-mani said, heading towards the bedroom with me still hanging over his shoulder.

"Oh shit, bitch, he about to give you that angry sex. You on your own, don't anybody want to hear that. Peace!" Tasha said and they all started grabbing their stuff and heading out the door.

"Really, bitches?" I said as they left closing the door behind them leaving me alone with Ky-mani.

"Ky-mani, put me down!" I said louder but he continued carrying me back to the bedroom. He pushed the door shut with his foot and dropped me on the bed. I tried to stand back up but he kneeled down in front of me and pushed me back down.

He held my arms down so I couldn't move and looked me in the eyes.

I wasn't a weak bitch by far. Other than the night I left Ky-mani's house after losing my job, I haven't cried once. Even after seeing the pics that Monae sent, I still wouldn't cry. But as I sat looking into Ky-mani's eyes, the man I loved more than anything in such a

40

short space of time, my tears flowed.

My heart yearned for him and pained at the same time over what had happened.

I pulled one of my hands out of his and wiped my tears away. He dropped his head and shook it.

"Baby, I swear I didn't sleep with Monae," he said lowly but I scoffed.

"You never told me you were going over there in the first place and I saw the pics Ky-mani so please rid me of that bs," I said, wiping my face again.

"Honey, I did not fuck Monae. You right I never told you I was going there but I was only supposed to be there for a minute getting Chyna together," he said but I ignored him. Sorting Chyna out but instead, you ended up laying pipe to Monae?

He pulled my face to look at him. "Honey, listen to me. Baby, if I did it I would have said I fucked up. I've never ever lied to you, Honey, no matter what. I told you from the jump, I ain't no liar. I'm a man about mine, my pop taught me to be a man no matter the consequences. I've never cheated on you, ma. Why would I do that? Why would I have waited all that time to make love to you and then go and cheat? Monae

41

ain't worth you, baby. I'm not a fool. I ain't fucked that bitch since she got pregnant with my son," he said, holding my hand on his heart.

"I told you about my past; I was honest about the women I had been with, about Angel, even though you could have left me but I refused to ever lie to you. And I'm not lying now, baby. I. Did. Not. Sleep. With. Monae," he said, staring me straight in my eyes.

"The pictures," I said lowly and he grabbed his phone.

"Look at the pictures, Honey," he said, trying to show me but I turned my head.

"You want me to relive that? I'll pass, thanks," I sniffled.

"Baby, trust me please," he said and I turned to look at him after a few seconds.

"Look at this pic," he said, showing me the one with him and her laying in the bed.

"Can't you see it's all wrong. First of all, I'm asleep, look at my face. So, I fucked her, put back on my boxers after to go sleep? For what? I ain't ever put back on clothes to sleep after you and I make love, have I?" he asked and I shook my head.

"Secondly, look at the bed I'm in. A princess bed. That's Chyna's room, why would I even think about fucking in my daughter's bed like that? And it's not broken? Come on, baby, you know how I get down. How can a child's bed take the weight of two grown adults fucking on it? Why would I need to be in Chyna's room in the first place? Why not fuck in Monae's room?" he asked and I looked at him.

"That's because I was lying down with Chyna, not Monae. I was in my boxers because I had been drinking and smoking with the boys so I couldn't get in her bed with my clothes. I fell asleep putting her to bed because she was having nightmares. That's why I was over there for Chyna, not Monae. After I fell asleep, she got in bed with me and took those pictures," he said but I still didn't say a word.

"These pics," he said, showing me the one with her sucking his dick and the one when she was just about to sit on it. I closed my eyes and tried to swallow the lump that formed.

"Look at me, Honey," he said but I couldn't because the tears were burning and if I did they would have fallen.

"Baby, please," he pleaded and when the sound of crying left my lips, I covered my mouth to stop it. My body shook as I cried silently into my hand.

"Shit, Honey baby, please," he pleaded again. I quickly pulled myself together and looked at him.

"I admit that was on me. I was asleep and thought it was you. I'm not even going to lie. But look here at my face," he zoomed in on it, in the last pic.

"As soon as I remembered I wasn't home, I woke my ass up. Look you can see I just woke up and look I'm mad. Why would I be mad if that's what I want or knew? That makes no sense. What would I be mad for, Honey, if I'm cheating? And it's not because of the camera because I hadn't even seen it. I didn't even know she had taken pics and posted until after I left and my momma called me," he said and I looked down at the pic.

I was so focused on seeing her dirty pussy about to sit on his dick that I never saw anything else but at that point, I saw his face clearly. And he had the meanest look on his face. What did he have to be mad about, he wanted pussy and she was giving it to him

44

right? So, what would he be mad about, unless he didn't want it?

You ever give pussy to a man who wants it and he looked angry? Even if he had a woman at home, his ass ain't going to be angry when he's about to fuck. That nigga is gone be smiling and feeling pleasure. But Ky-mani had a look of death on his face, not lust or pleasure.

"I pushed that bitch off not even a second after she took that pic when I got my focus. I woke up mad when I remembered that I wasn't home with my baby and knew it was her thot ass. But I promise you from my heart, Honey, I didn't fuck her. Baby, I love you from my soul, I would never ever do you dirty like that, ever. Please believe me," he said, holding my hand to his heart again.

I knew at that point, that I fucked up. I trusted Ky-mani and I knew if he had fucked up he would have told me the truth. No matter how much it hurt, he still would have told me. Even though I ran a part of me was willing to forgive purely for the fact that people fuck up sometimes and deserve a second chance. And if I could forgive Jerome why couldn't I

45

forgive Ky-mani? But as sure as I was that he truly loved me, I was sure that he never slept with Monae.

"I'm sorry," I said, breaking down again.

"Baby, it's ok, you have nothing to be sorry about. I'm sorry it came to this and that I ever went over there. I'm sorry you had to experience seeing that, Honey," he said, holding on to me.

He wiped my tears away and kissed me all over my face. "I missed you so much, baby. You are my life, Honey. I don't want anybody but you. Please believe me, baby, you complete me and make me whole. Don't ever leave me again, I can't function without you," he said, kissing me long and deep. Our tongues danced together as we rekindled ourselves as one.

He stood to his feet and took his clothes off. "Since your ass likes to run, I'm gonna give you something to make you run," he said.

I turned and tried to crawl up the bed but he grabbed my ankles.

"I'm sorry!" I laughed as he pulled me back down to him.

"Not yet you ain't," he laughed and pulled my jeans and panties off. He dropped to his knees and clamped his lips hard on my pussy.

"Shit!" I screamed out as he literally gnawed on my pussy. He wrapped his arms around my hips and pulled me further down the bed into his tongue. He pushed my top up exposing my breasts and I pulled it up over my head.

"

Ahhh, Ky-mani," I cried out. I sat up on my elbows and looked down.

His head was buried so deep in between my legs.

My legs started to tremble as he continued sucking everything out my pussy. I thought he would let up, but he continued relentlessly.

I dropped back on the bed and arched my back.

"Shit, Ky-mani, I can't," I stuttered. "I can't," I tried to say again but it was like words left my body.

He pushed my legs wide open as far as they could go and inserted a finger. He started massaging the walls of my pussy with his finger with his tongue going wild on my clit.

"Ahhh!!!" I screamed and tried to push his head up but he was stuck like glue to my pussy.

Damn, my nigga was trying to kill me with his tongue. I thought and squirmed.

"Ky-mani, please I can't handle it," I squirmed some more. But when he wrapped his lips tightly around my clit and popped it between his teeth, my body went wild.

"FUCK! Shiiiittttt!" I groaned and came so hard I thought my head was going to explode. But he wasn't done with my ass. With me still shaking from coming, he climbed on top of me, locked his legs with mine and gave me all of his dick.

"Ahhh," I grunted and he laughed. I tried to climb up the bed but he held my shoulders, keeping me in place.

"Uh huh, stay here and take this dick, baby," he said, thrusting deeply into me.
I couldn't even talk, he had my ass speaking in tongues. All I could do was drop my head to the side, bite down on my lip and moan.

"Damn, I missed you," Ky-mani hissed, dropping his head in my neck.

"Ohhh, baby. I missed you more." My body purred.

He fucked my ass really good into the next day. When he was done with me, my ass slept all the way home like a damn baby.

But when we got home, he made my ass remember who was the boss. My baby tapped my ass out!

****

Now that I was back, it was time to face Marco. I had done a lot of thinking and praying during the time that I was gone and I realized that God never made mistakes. If Marco continued to be in my life, I probably would have been dead by now but I wasn't because he made a selfless choice by leaving me.

That must have been hard for him to do especially as my momma told me how much he loved me and how I never slept at night as a baby unless I was on his chest. I couldn't hate him for that, he gave me a chance and I would forever love him for that.

49

Ky-mani took me to see him at his momma's house and as soon as I saw him, I fell into his arms and cried.

"I'm not angry anymore. I know you left because you loved me and I'm so sorry for hating you," I cried and he cried too.

"I have thought of you ever day, Honey, and I missed you so bad, baby. But to know you grew into such a beautiful woman, I am so proud of you, baby," he said, wiping my tears away.

"Do you still like Power Puff Girls?" he asked and we laughed so hard.

"Yep," I admitted and he laughed.

"I love you, baby girl."

"I love you too, Marco," I said and he kissed my cheek. I'm glad he didn't mention that whole calling him Marco thing but we needed time before I even thought of calling him daddy.

I turned to see Cameron looking at me; he went back to Atlanta for a while because his momma still lives out there. I walked over to him and we hugged.

"I always wanted a baby sister," he said and I laughed.

50

"Does that mean you're gonna stop with the whole baby brother shit now? I ain't the youngest anymore," Ricky said and we laughed.

"Sure thing – baby brother!" Cam said and we laughed.

"Ayo sis, be careful with that one," Cam said, pointing at Ky-mani. "You better be careful that some of his craziness doesn't rub off on your ass," he said and started laughing.

"Voice note, my nigga," Ky-mani said and Cam stopped laughing instantly.

Ky-mani pulled me away from Cam and hugged me. "I love you, baby," he smiled and kissed me.

"I love you too, baby," I smiled and hugged him tightly.

I thanked the Lord for giving me a good man and for bringing my daddy to me.

Life was perfect!

Chapter Four

Honey

Two months later

"Bitch, is your ass on birth control yet?" Tasha asked me as we sat munching away on lunch.

"No, but I made an appointment with the clinic," I said and she looked up at me.

"So y'all still playing pussy roulette I see," she said, laughing.

That's what she called the pulling out method that Ky-mani and I had been using when we either couldn't wait to get a condom or we ran out. But lately, I noticed that we did that more often instead of even getting a condom.

So far we had been lucky, four months in and no pregnancy but I was done taking chances. With the two kids, Angel five months pregnant, his businesses, him still working the streets waiting on whoever to strike again, and let's not forget the new house, my baby didn't have time for anything else and especially not a baby. And my ass damn sure wasn't ready for that.

I was still living in Ky-mani's house and I was so busy building up a client list to eventually open my own accountant business, I wouldn't even have the time for a baby anyway. Plus, I had a few viewings for apartments and I was yet to tell Ky-mani that I did. Life was hectic but we were happy. None of our asses needed a baby thrown in.

My appointment for the shots wasn't until next week but I gave my number to the office and asked them to call me if they had any cancellations; the sooner I could get back on them, the better.

When I finished my lunch with Tasha, I dropped her off and headed home.

I was surprised to see that Ky-mani was home.

"Hey, baby," I said, kissing him passionately on the lips.

"Hey, my Queen, how you doing?" he asked, pulling me down on his lap.

"I'm good. I didn't expect to see you," I said

smiling.

"I was missing you so I brought my work home with me," he winked.

"Ok. Well while you're doing that, I'm going to put dinner on," I smiled and kissed him.

"Oh before you do, I need you to look at something for me," he said, handing me a catalog.

"Pick a bathroom suite you like," he said before looking over something else on his desk.

"For what?" I asked confused.

"For our adjoining bathroom. I've asked them to change its current one so we can have a his and hers theme. I know how you like to be in the mirror," he laughed.

"But I want you to pick one you like since your ass gone be in it more than me," he laughed again.

Oh my god, his and hers bathroom. That was exactly what I didn't want. He had to move and because I'm here he feels like he had to take me with him. I never wanted him to feel obligated or stuck with me. I know he wanted us to live together but it's early days now so I know he's happy but a year down the line he won't be.

Eventually, people's habits and behaviors can

54

annoy us even if we loved them. He was already comparing how long I took in the bathroom compared to him and although he didn't mind now, later down the line he might. I didn't want us to get like that with each other. Jerome and my relationship changed after we started living together and I don't want that with me and Ky-mani.

Yes, we lived together now but it felt like I was still staying with him until I moved and he did. But him installing his and her bathrooms would be us living together, sharing a home and I didn't think he was truly ready for that.

"Ahh right," I chuckled. "You know you don't have to do that," I cleared my throat. "A normal bathroom is fine, no need to go through all that trouble of his and hers," I said and he looked up at me.

He stared at me without saying a word. After a few seconds, he gave a small chuckle and went back to work.

"I was just saying. Saves all that trouble," I said quietly.

"Yeah, maybe you're right," he said, without looking up at me.

"I'm gonna go start dinner," I said, putting the catalog down.

"Yeah you do that," he said, grabbing the catalog and throwing it in the trash.

I wanted to say something but I didn't. I just left his office and went to the kitchen.

When we ate dinner, he was talking to me but not really. It wasn't a genuine smile or laughter; I could see his little eyes staring off into space like he was thinking something else but he never said what it was. I knew it was from what I had said because he was fine up until that point and when he left out earlier in the day.

I wanted to bring it up so I could try to explain but I just knew in my heart it wouldn't have ended well.

Ky-mani and I had been together for four months and in those four months, we had disagreed on many things but never argued.

I could feel one in the air brewing. I could smell it like when the air around you change and you know it's about to rain.

I could feel the storm cloud in the room and I

56

wasn't trying to get wet in that bitch.

Maybe another day when I was prepared, with my umbrella and shit, so to speak.

The only thing I knew would prevent any arguing from starting was sleep.

The quicker I slept, the quicker it would be tomorrow and a new day. I didn't mind if we argued tomorrow but it just couldn't be tonight.

So, after we cleaned away, I took my ass upstairs to shower and get in the bed. I was surprised to see him sitting on the bed when I came out. He went back into his office as I came up, so I thought he would've stayed down there for a while and then I could sleep before he came up. Or at least pretend to be. You know how we females do sometimes.

When he looked up and saw me, he threw down the remote that he had in his hand and smiled at me as he passed to go to the bathroom himself.

I put lotion on my skin, threw on some panties and a night shirt. I didn't even bother with the kindle for tonight just in case that triggered his ass in some way.

I switched the lights off, climbed in bed on my

back, and shut my eyes.

I opened them when I felt the blanket being pulled off of me 10 minutes later and my legs being pulled. I looked up and Ky-mani had a huge grin on his face standing down at my feet, wearing nothing but a damn erection.

He licked his lips and parted my legs.

Ok, he's not mad, just horny. I smiled at him when he climbed on top of me.

He slammed his lips down onto mine and I sucked his tongue into my mouth like a piece of fruit.

"Mmmm," he moaned as he pulled my nightshirt up and over my head. He kissed me all over my face before finding my lips again.

He grabbed my breasts and squeezed them letting out another soft moan.

He kissed down to my neck and sucked on it for a minute; I knew his ass was leaving a mark. He then moved further down my body and did the same thing on my left breast. He sucked the top of it like he was trying to draw blood.

That nigga was leaving marks everywhere his

mouth touched including my thighs. He smiled when he finished leaving his 'I was here' marks and I shook my head at him.

He went back to kissing and licking on my breasts and pulled down my panties at the same time. He licked his thumb and brushed it over my pussy in an upward motion. Before opening my legs and trailing his tongue in a straight line from the very bottom of my pussy, just before my ass started, to the top where my Brazilian wax started.

He started eating my pussy like he didn't just finish eating a goddamn feast.

He devoured my pussy making me come over and over again.

Fuck me! I thought shaking my head. He almost tapped my ass out with just his tongue game.

He kissed me and slid his dick up in my guts. He pushed his head into my neck and dug his dick deep like he was tunneling for gold or something.

"Damn, baby, you have the best pussy ever. I can't get enough," he whispered in my ear.

"Baby, you got the best dick ever," I threw right back at him because he did. He had my ass under a spell with his dick game. Nigga knew how to sling pipe that was for sure.

He dug his hands underneath me and grabbed my ass. He went in for the kill pounding away making my eyes roll back. I was twisting and turning, curling my toes enjoying this dick. I was enjoying it some much I almost forgot he needed to pull out.

I was surprised when he was still deep in me. I could feel his legs trembling so I knew he was almost there. Usually, he would pull out and finish on my stomach or thighs. But the death grip he had on my ass cheeks let me know he was rooted in that pussy.

"Babe, don't forget to pull out," I whispered and squirmed trying to get him up.

He let go of my ass and hugged onto my shoulders, keeping me in place and his dick deep inside. "Babe," I said and he kissed me and continued to thrust.

"Oh shit," he grunted against my lips and his body shook.

"Bae, you gotta pull out," I squirmed again.

"Mmm hmmm I will. It just feels so good,

baby. One more minute," he groaned, rotating his hips into me.

"Shit!!!" He cried out with his head back and I felt his dick trembling but he kept right on thrusting.

"Bae, pull out!" I screamed and he pulled out of me.

"Fuck, Honey!" he grunted. He grabbed his dick and seeds and hauled his ass in the bathroom, slamming the door behind him.

He had never caught himself that close before. Was he really going to pull out if I didn't yell at him? It didn't feel like he was.

A few seconds later and he came back in with a damp cloth for me. He handed it to me and picked up his boxers.

"What was up with that, Honey?" he asked as I wiped myself clean. I looked up and he was angry.

So much for not arguing tonight!

I pulled the blanket up over my body and he shook his head at me.

"You said you were gonna pull out and it didn't feel like you were," I said.

"So and what if I didn't?"

"You know what, Ky-mani."

"Why the fuck is the Franklin Clinic calling your ass?" he snarled.

"Because I made an appointment for the Depo shots," I folded my arms.

"For what!?!" he yelled.

"Birth control, Ky-mani."

"I know what the fuck it is! I ain't a retarded nigga. You don't need that shit and that's exactly why I canceled that appointment," he said and grabbed a blunt from the top of the dresser and flamed it up.

"You did what?!" I yelled.

"You heard me. Your ass isn't deaf. You ain't getting no motherfucking shots, Honey."

"I am, Law!" I said and he shot his eyes at me.

"What? It's obvious I'm dealing with Law here," I said and he laughed.

"It is clear to see that this pulling out shit isn't going to work. You cut it close tonight."

"Close to what, Honey?"

"You know damn well my ass will get pregnant if you don't pull out so stop playing."

"And so what if you do!!! You're my woman,

Honey, so motherfucking what!"

"Ky-mani, you already have a baby on the way with Angel. You don't need anymore."

"Did I ask your ass anything about Angel? We ain't talking about that bitch," he said.

"Ain't you my woman, Honey?" he asked and I nodded my head. "Don't we live together? Well for now," he said and I looked at him. "What the fuck are you looking for apartments for? What, you thought my ass didn't know?" he said, but I didn't even have an answer for him about that, so I went back to what he said before.

"Ky-mani, I don't want to have a baby yet," I admitted.

"What a baby or my baby, Honey?" he puffed on the blunt.

"I didn't say that, stop putting words in my mouth."

"Honey, I'm doing things for you I ain't ever done before in my life. There're a thousand bitches out there that want what you got! Monae's ass is jumping through all kinds of hoops to get my ass, but you got me spilling my goddamn seeds pulling out my pussy!!!

You got these motherfucking thots out here carrying my seeds but your ass doesn't want to!" he yelled.

"Yes, Ky-mani, because I fucked those bitches and got them pregnant with your seeds, didn't I?" I yelled back.

He outed the blunt and stood back in front of me pulling the blanket off me again.

"Fuck this! You ain't going on no Depo shots and I ain't pulling out shit. If it happens, it motherfucking happens," he said, grabbing my legs, climbing on top of me, and shoving his dick in me.

He pushed his tongue roughly into my mouth and started to thrust fast in and out of me.

"Ky-mani, stop! So, you just gonna take it and get my ass pregnant?" I said and he looked down at me.

"Take it? Honey, I," he said and then he let me go.

I jumped up out the bed and grabbed my night shirt. I ran into my closet and he grabbed me.

"Let me go!" I screamed.

"Baby, I'm sorry. I didn't mean to hurt you," he

said, hugging onto my body with his head down in my chest. "It's just you got my head fucked up about not wanting my baby and I wasn't thinking straight. I would never intentionally hurt you like that, Honey, I love you. You don't need to leave Ma, I will. It's obvious you don't want my ass," he said, letting me go and grabbing a suitcase.

"Ky-mani, I do want you. I love you. I'm just not ready for a baby yet. There's so much going on at the moment," I cried but he continued to grab his clothes and drop them in the suitcase.

"Ky-mani, please talk to me!" I yelled at him.

"What do you want me to say, Honey? You want me to lie to your ass and say this don't bother me when it does? I want you to have my baby. I'm ready for it but you got me making sure I don't get you pregnant and you've been looking for apartments, it's obvious you don't want what I want," he said.

"Please stay, Ky-mani, don't leave me," I cried.

"Honey, I'm not going to accept you going on the shots and I ain't going to use no condoms or pull out. Call it selfish but I want you and I want to have a baby with you. Are you willing to make love to me

65

now and allow me to do that?" he asked and I shook my head no.

"But you were planning and ready to give that dirty dick motherfucker a baby but not me! And you happily lived with his no-good ass!!! Maybe I need to cheat on your ass, get a few bitches pregnant before you will really want my ass!" he said and I slapped him across the face.

He looked at me angry with nostril flaring and his jaw clenched tight.

"Fuck this!" he said and hauled his ass out of the house, slamming the door hard on the way out.

I listened as he broke some shit outside before hearing his car door slam and tires screech as he drove away.

Chapter Five

Law

I know what you're thinking. Was I really trying to impregnate Honey? And the simple answer was yes. You may hate me now or think I was being selfish but I was. Like I said I was a thug, not a liar.

The truth was I was sick and tired of Monae and Angel's asses. They were driving me insane with Monae trying to fuck my life up with Honey every goddamn chance she got and Angel texting all kind of shit throwing in my face that she was pregnant and not Honey.

Deep down inside I just knew that if Honey was to get pregnant it would all end and we could be happy. After all, if they believed they should have me because of the kids then wouldn't Honey be just as entitled being pregnant for me? Sure, I didn't need any more kids at the moment since Angel's ass was

67

pregnant but you don't know what it was like, seeing these women that I didn't love or want, having my kids when the woman I did love and want didn't.

I wanted to share that special moment with Honey. I didn't want any more kids if they weren't with her but here I was having one with another woman. All I wanted was to be left alone and to be happy with Honey. If that made me wrong, well I was wrong.

Honey was on one, a pure determination not to get pregnant. We started off not using anything because she wasn't due any shots yet since she was taking them when she was with Killa. So, there wasn't any chance of pregnancy. But a month after, when she was due, we started using condoms. There were a few times when we either were not patient enough to get one or we ran out, that I went in raw but she always made sure I pulled out.

At first, I was ok with it but as time went on, I started thinking more and more about her having my baby. Especially after the stunt Monae pulled. I knew her ass would sit down somewhere with Honey being pregnant. So, I made it my routine to use the pulling out method simply because I hoped that once or twice,

Honey would be so caught up in the dick that she would forget and I would get to release my seeds in her.

But every damn time, and I meant every fucking time, she would scream out and remind me to pull out.

I did it to please her but that day something just snapped in me. And let's not forget that she was looking at apartments! The thing I loved about Honey was that she wasn't a sneaky bitch. I never had to wonder what she was doing; she was open with me at all times. There was no code on her cell or IPad, so that was how I saw that she was looking at apartments, she even had a meeting to view two. Yeah, I know she would have told me but the fact is she shouldn't have been looking!

I had done everything in my power to make Honey feel and know that she was home and not sleeping over or staying over for the moment.

I always referred to it as home or our house. She had her own keys and fob for the gate. I had the closet remodeled so she would have her own side complete with shoe racks and full-length mirrors, a vanity area, and an area for all her hair equipment to be kept.

But no matter what, she apologized when she left her IPad around the house, always said she was in the way or constantly said my house.

Did she really   think I was purchasing the house just for me?! She gave no input for it, everything I asked her about the house and what she liked or what we should do with it, I was told whatever I thought or liked.

I couldn't help but lose my cool when I handed her the catalog to pick out a his and hers bathroom design and she practically told me to leave it how it was. I couldn't understand why bitches that I just fucked, didn't feel for, didn't want, never spoke to more than asking for some pussy, damn near ignored unless it had to do with pussy; wanted nothing more than to live with me and have my babies.

But here I was a street nigga who had a different woman every day, who didn't believe in having one woman, who never loved, never dated, never wanted a woman in my life period, changed all that for Honey and still she was telling me no! I gave her all that Killa didn't but she lived with him and planned on having kids with him?! Of course, I couldn't

70

understand.

I knew what time it was and I knew I was going to get into it with her because I was fuming sitting at dinner but I kept a cool face. I already knew either me or her was going to leave at the end of it. But a part of me hoped she wouldn't have done what she did.

But there I was deep in my pussy, fucking the shit out of her until she couldn't even talk. I was determined and doing my thing and then she yells out over and over again telling me to pull out. That shit got to me and fucked up my nut.

Why was she so persistent about not getting pregnant and moving out?!

Obviously, Honey didn't love me like I loved her, so I had to bow out as much as I loved her. She was hurting me and didn't even know it. I was doing everything in my power to keep us together and she was doing everything in her power to separate our lives.

She begged me to stay but for what? So, I could continue to fuck her and pull out or watch her go down to the clinic to get a drug that would stop her from ever getting pregnant for me? To watch her move out into her own apartment like a slap in the face?

Granted she moved in because of what happened, but I asked before we knew what happened. But now I was thinking that maybe she would have said no if her apartment wasn't destroyed.

I don't know what Honey wanted. I thought it was me and she said it was, and a part of me believed that. But why in God's name did she want to move out, if I'm what she wanted and she wanted to be there. And if she didn't want to be there…why?

I wasn't shit though because I left hickeys all over her damn body on purpose. I knew things would have ended like that, I couldn't leave my seeds behind so I left my insurance. Any nigga who approached her would have seen my marks and known to back the fuck up.

I wasn't a stupid man; I was angry and in my feelings but I knew weren't any females out there like Honey and I knew I would never find another woman like her. So, I damn sure wasn't leaving her out there for the wolves.

She was angry and I was angry after she slapped the shit outta me; but all we needed was some time and all would be good.

72

***

Almost two weeks later

Ok, how much time did Honey need? Her ass was still not talking to me. I apologized a thousand times but she still didn't want to know. And she was still banning my ass from coming to the crib like really?

I missed her something hard but she wasn't trying to entertain my ass. I logged into my ADT security system on my computer and saw Honey sitting on the couch reading. I loved her so much and I missed her even more. I don't know why but I decided to call her.

I laughed when I watched her pick up the cell, saw it was me calling, and shook her head.

"Hello, Ky-mani," she said and I smiled.

"Hey, baby," I said.

"Honey," she corrected me.

"My bad, Honey," I accepted.

"Why are you calling me, Ky-mani?"

"To see how you are."

73

"I'm fine," she answered back quickly.

"What are you doing, ma?" I asked, smiling because I just knew her ass would lie just so she wouldn't have to tell me.

"I'm out, Ky-mani," she said and I smiled and shook my head.

"Oh yeah? Where?"

"Just out, Ky-mani."

"Oh ok. You sure you're not just laying up on the couch?" I asked, fighting hard not to laugh.

"No, Ky-mani, I'm not. In fact, I'm out on a date," she said and I laughed.

"Is that so?" I chuckled.

"Yep. So, I have to go, it's rude me being on the phone with you," she said.

"Yeah ok. So, if I went by the house, you wouldn't be there?"

"No I wouldn't but you cannot go there. Your ass wanted to go so stay gone. But I'm going to go and enjoy my date. Goodbye, Ky-mani," she said and hung up.

All I could do was laugh when she jumped up to check I wasn't outside before climbing back on the couch to read.

I continued to watch her as she walked around

74

the house cleaning as she always did. When she changed her clothes to work out, I couldn't control myself. I missed her so fucking much. Her beautiful body shone like the fucking sun as she stripped down to just her panties.

Goddamn, Honey. I thought as I grabbed my throbbing dick.

Her breasts looked so damn good and the bikini style black lace panties she had on made me lose my mind.

I wanted to go into that house and fuck the shit outta her. I missed the taste of her body. Fuck porn, my baby was so much more. She had me in my office ready to bust a goddamn nut.

She pulled on her working out clothes and went into the living room to workout. No matter what, my baby kept herself tight.

I watched her do a couple positions before turning the security feed off, I couldn't watch any more.

I felt like a sucker but not at the same time. I stood by how I felt but then I wished I didn't leave

like that. But I did mainly out of shame and anger.
Shame from when she said the words take it.

I've never had to take pussy if anything I would
say my ass had been raped and molested by bitches
grabbing my dick and forcing they mouth on it.
Waiting for me to be drunk and then trying to fuck me.

But when Honey said those words I felt
ashamed. How could things have escalated to the
point that I grabbed her like that and forced my dick
in her? My pops would have been ashamed.

But then I felt anger too, anger that she drove me
to that point with all of that goddamn 'pull out bae'
shit she was hollering. Like what the fuck, I was Ky-
mani Law Parker! I was the motherfucking King
around this bitch, why the fuck wouldn't she want my
seeds? I wasn't a cocky nigga, I didn't need to be, but
I knew my ass was fine. Long before I had money, I
had bitches at my face, the money only added to my
appeal. I had more money than I could motherfucking
count and I was a damn good man to Honey. I knew
my ass was a good father, my pops was and I just
followed his suit.

So why the fuck was she carrying on like that?

I wanted answers and I wanted them now. I felt like going to the house and demanding she told me what was up? She needed to explain that shit to me. I wanted to go over there so bad but instead, I grabbed a bottle of Hennessy and sat all in my feelings and drank.

A few hours passed and my ass was still in my office thinking and drinking. I was drunk but still able to drive. Since I walked out the house, I had been staying in The Marriott Hotel because my house wasn't quite finished yet. I jumped in the car and headed there.

I don't know why but something came over me and I spun my car around and headed towards Honey. I just needed to see her face, see if we could at least try to talk things over.

But when I pulled up, something wasn't right. There was a car out front that I didn't recognize and instantly I knew a nigga was in my house with my woman.

I was angry but I shouldn't have been because I walked out on her but she didn't have to do me like that already.

Two motherfucking weeks! She wasn't serious.

I grabbed my gun and tucked it in my back as I climbed out of the car. I pushed up the car door gently so it wouldn't make a sound.

I used my keys and entered the house. All the lights were off downstairs except two little lights flicking; one from the living room TV and one coming from the kitchen. I crept to the living room and saw a blanket on the couch and two empty glasses next to a bottle of wine.

I looked up the spiral staircase and was about to head up to the bedroom when I heard a bottle rattle in the kitchen.

Nigga done gone fucked my girl and now his ass was hungry. I thought. Ma must have fucked his ass good.

Whenever Honey put that pussy on me, I either fell right asleep or my ass got hungry after the workout she would give my ass. I felt like crying and vomiting all at the same time. Ma was killing a nigga.

I drew my gun and crept to the kitchen with my gun held down by my side. I pushed the door slowly and there stood a tall nigga in fucking basketball shorts bent over with his head in my fucking refrigerator.

Oh, hell no nigga, first your ass was in my pussy now it's in my refrigerator? Going too fucking far now. I thought as I got up behind him and put my gun to his head.

"Nigga, you come into my house fuck my woman and eat my fucking food!" I said in a high whisper.

"I should blow your fucking head off right now. You disrespected me, nigga," I gritted my teeth.

"My nigga look," he said with his hands held out.

"Nigga, shut your mouth! Honey is my woman, nigga! Ain't no one fucking her but my ass!"

"G, for real my…"

"Shut your ass up. Let's go outside, my friend," I said, tapping his head with the gun. I wasn't about to kill this dude with Honey in the house.

"Yo, G, for real my name is Troy Johnson. Johnson my nigga!" he said.

"What you say to me?" I asked. *Isn't Honey's name Johnson?*

"Yo, cuz, who you talking to – oh my God, Ky-mani, what are you doing to my cousin?" I turned as I heard Honey yell.

I quickly dropped my gun and pushed it back on my waist.

"Ky-mani, are you crazy?! You snuck into the house and pulled a gun on my cousin? I told you Troy was coming. You're the one who suggested he stay here remember?" she said with her hands on her hips.

Shit she did say her cousin was coming into town for a few days so I told her to let them stay here, but she never said it was a nigga!

"My bad. But you never said it was a dude," I said, rubbing my head.

"Yes I did, but your ass wasn't paying attention. And am I only going to have female cousins, Ky-mani?" she rolled her eyes at me.

"My bad, my nigga," I said, shaking Troy's hand.

"Oh, I'm good, nigga. Any dude who's willing to kill a nigga over my cousin, I fucking love," he said, laughing and I laughed too.

"Nigga, you got my ass shook though I ain't gone lie. But I love it. At least I know she got a real man out here looking after her," he dapped me. "But you know I taught her ass how to fight," he smiled.

"Yo, you're the Cuz who did?" I asked and he nodded his head. "My nigga, you did well. My baby can throw those hands. She out here knocking bitches out with one punch," I said, smiling hard and he laughed.

"That's my Cuz," he laughed.

You would think that I didn't just have a gun to his head. My man was cool, though. He knew what time it was, I loved his cousin and any nigga was getting dropped over her ass.

"Ahem!" I heard her say and we instantly stopped talking.

"Yeah I'mma step out," Troy said to me.

81

"Yeah you do that," Honey said to him with her arms folded. He dapped me up and disappeared out of the kitchen.

Honey looked so beautiful with a mean mug on her face. "Ky-mani, what are you doing here?"

"I came to see you."

"For what?" she frowned.

"To apologize, baby."

"Ok, for what?" she said, tapping her foot at me.

"For everything, Honey. I'm sorry."

She rolled her eyes and shook her head at me.

"Let me stop you right there. Don't come in here apologizing and you don't know what for. I ain't no common ass bitch, don't give me any half bullshit apology. Don't be sorry because you wanna be forgiven. Tell my ass what you apologizing for. And if you don't know, figure that shit out. You come in here and almost kill my cousin over nothing," she shook her head.

"How was I supposed to know he was your cousin? I don't know if your ass moved on already since your ass is done with me."

"So what, you came in here to kill whatever nigga you thought I had around me? Staking your claim like you did with my body? Leaving all those

82

hickeys on me, I know why you did that," she said.

Damn, my baby wasn't any fool. I wanted every motherfucker who looked at her to know my ass was there. I sucked all over her fine ass body.

"All of that was unnecessary but clearly you don't know who you're dealing with. I'm going to take my ass back to bed and you can go on wherever you came from." She turned to walk away.

"Honey, so you not going to help a nigga out?" I asked because she was right. I didn't know what I was apologizing for exactly because everything else I did apologize for wasn't it, so I was just sorry at that point. But my baby was a queen and her ass wasn't accepting shit. But she could at least point me in the right direction.

"Yeah I will help you out," she said smiling. "The door is that way, let yourself out and be sure to close it on the way out," she smiled and walked away.

"Honey," I said but she didn't come back.

I walked out of the kitchen and watched her sexy ass disappear up the stairs.

"Good luck, cousin in law. The women in my family are boss bitches. Remember I told you that. And her and my sister are the worse ones," he said, patting my shoulder.

***

Three days later

I still didn't know what to apologize for. I called Honey and apologized for everything I did that night, but she still said I was missing something. She had my ass tapped out. Even her cousin, Troy, tried to get that information out of her but ma wasn't biting. She knew what we were up to.

And I wasn't even trying to ask her crazy ass girls shit. We all knew they wouldn't have told my ass anyway.

Maybe I just needed to lay this pipe on her ass. That's what she needed, this dick in her life. I was sitting up in my hotel room with Ricky. The other niggas had dates except us two. Sydney was on vacation with her momma, so Ricky was lonely.

I just wanted to see Honey and make love to

her, even if just once. I needed my baby. Ricky was about to roll out, so I thought I would follow him out and go see Honey. But if her cousin was still there, I knew she wouldn't fuck me with him being there. And knowing Honey, if I called her to ask, her smart ass would just tell me he was so I wouldn't come over.

So, I grabbed my cell so I could look for myself on the security system. I logged in and looked in every room but there was no sign of him. I decided to look in my room to see what Honey was doing and I lost my fucking cool.

There was a nigga standing in my room with her laid back in the bed, and it wasn't her cousin! This nigga started rubbing on her legs and moved his hand up until he reached her nightshirt and pushed it up exposing her panties.

"WHAT THE FUCK!?! Nah, Honey, fuck this!" I spat, throwing my cell across the floor.

"What's up, cuz?" Ricky said, jumping to his feet.

I grabbed my gun and my keys as Ricky picked up my phone.

"Honey, has some nigga in my house, looking

85

like they about to fuck. I'm not having that, she needs to fucking get to her senses now; I ain't playing no more," I headed for the door. "That nigga ain't fucking shit!" I growled as I raced down to my car.

"I'm rolling wit you, my nigga, for real," Ricky said, checking his gun.

The hotel was about 10 minutes from my house but my ass got there in like three with me doing over a hundred on the dash.

I grabbed my gun and we rolled up to the house. I rushed in with Ricky on my tail. We went straight up the stairs to my room. The door was partially closed and I could hear this nigga moaning. Y'all know I blew my fucking top. I made Ricky stay outside because he didn't need to see his sister naked and I pushed the door open with my gun up.

I damn near lost my mind as I saw this nigga gnawing on my pussy. He had a fucking finger in her pussy and was eating her like he was finishing a fucking pot of yogurt. Honey was butt ass naked with her legs spread. This nigga stood to his feet and went to climb his naked ass on my woman but I pounced on his ass.

"Motherfucker, I wish you would fuck my woman," I said, grabbing him back and pushing my gun in his face.

I looked down and Honey didn't even flinch.

"Honey, for real! You about to fuck a nigga in my bed!? Get your ass up. Your ass ain't sleeping!" I yelled.

She thought my ass was stupid about her playing sleep.

"Honey!" I yelled again but she still didn't get up, nor did she try to cover her naked ass.

"She asleep, nigga. I drugged her." this motherfucker said.

"Nigga, what you just say?!" I started hyperventilating.

"I knocked her out, Law. She ain't gone wake up," he said.

This nigga knew who I was and still did that shit?!

I struck that nigga in his face with my gun. His shit busted wide open. I cut on the light and sure enough, she was out cold. I threw a blanket over her to cover her up and called Ricky into the room.

"Motherfucker, are you raping my wife?!" I yelled in his bloodied face and he nodded. This nigga actually nodded his head like it was ok.

I blacked out and started whooping this motherfucker's ass. I kicked and stomped his ass out. Ricky continued to whoop his ass as I ran over to Honey.

"Honey!" I shook her. "Baby, get up please," I continued to shake her. I rushed back over to the dude and started beating his ass again.

"He told me to," he groaned and I stopped stomping him. Ricky yoked his ass up and made him stand.

"Motherfucker, you best tell me everything or I'mma blow your motherfucking head off! And don't miss out a single thing," I said, aiming my gun at his face.

"I will tell you everything, Law, because I respect you. You the king for real, my nigga."

"Motherfucker, you know who I am but you still came into my house, drugged my wife, and tried to fuck her but you respect me, nigga?!"

"It's nothing personal, Law, I needed the money. There's a nigga called The Don; I ain't never seen him nor do I know where he lay his head at. But I know he's gunning for you. He wants it all. He was the one who sent those young niggas to kidnap you and your woman. He called me offered me twenty thou' to come in here and fuck your wife. I was supposed to take pictures and send them to you," he slurred.

I was so mad my chest was heaving.

"How did you get in here without setting the alarms off?"

"He gave me the code," he said, swaying on his feet.

"What the fuck you say?! That nigga has the code to my crib?" I asked and he nodded.

"How?"

"He said someone in your camp was a snake and gave it to him," he said and Ricky and I looked at each other then back at him.

"What you do to my wife, motherfucker? Did you fuck her?" My hand shook.

"No. I didn't."

"Nigga, did you put your dick in my wife!!!" I

roared and grabbed his throat and pressed my gun to his cheek.

"No, I swear. I did eat her pussy but I didn't fuck her, you stopped me before I could. I didn't fuck her," he said staggering.

"Is she going to be hurt from whatever you did to her?"

"No, but she will be out for a few hours, a day maybe," he said. "Are you gonna let me go? I told you everything I know," he said with his hands up.

"Yeah I'mma let you go, nigga...straight to hell, motherfucker!" I said, letting off a shot to his face. The bullet hit his cheek blowing a hole in it.

Ricky busted a shot to his stomach and we aired out our guns in that bitch, emptying our clips.

"We need to move to our safe house. Everybody! Monae, the kids and even Angel's ass," I said tucking the gun behind my back. I checked on Honey again and made sure she was breathing.

I pulled out my cell to call the others but no one answered, I guess the pussy was too sweet.

90

I called my momma and let her know to get out with the girls, Aunt Ruth, and Unc.

Ricky and I grabbed suitcases and grabbed all off Honey's and my shit throwing them inside. I grabbed all my files from my office and everything from the safes. We loaded up my car with everything inside save the furniture and equipment.

"Get the girls and kids, Ricky, and meet me at the house. I'mma bring Honey to the hospital and make sure she straight. I'll be there ASAP," I said and we dapped each other up.

He jumped in his car and sped off.
I quickly ran up to Honey. She was still knocked out. I throw some clothes on her and carried her out to my car. I strapped her in the front passenger seat and lowered it so she was laying back. I locked my car and ran back into the house.

I started dowsing the house in gas. That nigga broke into my home and tried to rape my wife, I would never set foot back in that house again.

I poured the rest of the gas on that nigga's body

and lit his ass up. I quickly ran my ass out of the house shutting the door behind me.

I climbed in my car and drove off towards Miami where our safe house was. It was a house that Ricky and I bought for our mommas. Nobody but us knew the address.

As I drove I prayed to God I didn't really have a snake in my camp. Maybe they were watching Honey and saw her enter the code but a snake would be fucking devastating because only my niggas know that bitch and Honey.

But I don't know who this nigga, The Don, was but he just fucked with the wrong one. They called me Law, nigga!!!

Chapter Six

Honey

I opened my eyes and I was in the hospital. I don't know why or even how I got there. I closed my eyes and tried to remember something but the only thing I did was waking up feeling someone's hand on my mouth and then feeling sleepy.

I lifted my head and looked around the room. I was surprised to see Ky-mani lying back asleep in a chair. "Ky-mani," I called him and his eyes popped open.

"Why am I in the hospital?" I asked.

"Because your hard-headed ass doesn't listen! If your ass just let me back in the house, none of this shit would be happening!" he yelled at me.

"Ky-mani, you fucking left, I didn't send your ass out. You left because your spoiled ass couldn't get your own way, so don't spin shit on me!" I yelled back.

"Yeah, but I came back and you were on some

93

bullshit! So, niggas took that as a fucking invitation to
break into my house and try to rape you!" he yelled
and tears rolled down my face.

I laid back down and the tears rolled down into
my ears. Ky-mani came and stood by the bed.

"Did they do something to me?! Oh my god!" I
cried my eyes out.

"Ma, he didn't touch you. I stopped him, ok? I
promise he didn't rape you but he almost did," he
said, holding my hand.

"So why am I here then?" I sniffled and wiped
my face.

"Because he drugged you and I wasn't sure with
what or what it would do to you. But you're good, Ma.
The doctor said it didn't do anything to you but made
you sleep," he said. "What happened? Did you see
anyone around you? Did anything suspicious happen
since I was gone?" he asked and I shook my head.

"No, Ky-mani, my cousin was over we just
went out and went straight back home. After he left I
was home all day, no one came, nothing out of the
ordinary. Until I woke up with someone in my room.
He said he was gone fuck me good and then he
covered my mouth. I tried to fight but it was like I

couldn't move. He pulled my night shirt up and then I blacked out," I said, crying again.

Maybe Ky-mani was right and him not being around wasn't the best idea especially after nearly getting kidnapped, but at the end of the day he left when I begged him to stay, so he couldn't put it all on me.

"Ky-mani, are you sure he didn't do anything to me?" I shook. I would hate to have been raped, but I would rather know if I was.

"Ma, I promise you with everything in me, he didn't rape you. I ain't gone lie he had his mouth on you but that was it," he said and I felt so dirty and ashamed, but more ashamed that Ky-mani had to see that.

I was crying moderately but when the door opened and Momma Doreen walked in I cried harder.

"Oh, baby, you ok?" she said, hugging me allowing me to cry on her shoulder.

"It's all my fault. I feel so dirty and ashamed," I whispered and she kissed my cheek.

"It wasn't your fault; there are some cruel motherfuckers out there," she said hugging me tightly.

"Marco is going out his head. Wanna kill everybody around him," she said and I laughed.

"I told Unc she got a man who can defend her. He tripping," Ky-mani said.

"I do not! You're not my man, Ky-mani. You made that very clear when you walked out on me," I said and Momma Doreen started laughing.

"See this the bullshit I be talking about! You better stop playing with me, Honey. Your ass is mine, pussy too," he said.

"Excuse me, my ass nor my cookies belong to you. I'm the boss of my body," I corrected his ass.

"Yeah, you weren't saying that shit when I laid this pipe on your ass, talking about 'yes, Ky-mani, you got the best dick ever.' Fuck outta here. You are my girl, I ain't playing with your ass," he said and jumped back on the chair.

"Ky-mani, leave that girl alone with all that mess," his momma said, pouring me a glass of water.

I looked over at Ky-mani and he was scowling at me. I folded my arms across my chest and rolled my eyes at him.

He sucked his teeth and jumped up. "Stop fucking with me, Honey," he said before he walked out of the room slamming the door.

Momma Doreen and I looked at each other and laughed.

The doctor came in and checked me over. He assured me that the drug didn't affect me in any kind of way. I was relieved to know that Ky-mani ordered a nurse to examine me to make sure I definitely wasn't penetrated front or back and I wasn't. He signed my discharge papers and told me I was free to go.

Momma Doreen handed me some clothes and I went into the bathroom to change. When I came out, Ky-mani was sitting on the bed. I came out of the room and walked right passed him without saying a word.

"So you can't see my ass?" he said but I didn't answer him.

He chuckled and pulled my bag from my hand and opened the door for us to leave.

When we got outside, I looked around but didn't recognize where I was.

"Um, Momma Doreen, what part of Chicago is this?" I asked and she laughed.

"We not in Chicago anymore, baby, we in Miami," she said.

"Why?"

"Because niggas are knowing the code to my crib, that's how homeboy got in without setting off the alarm. I didn't know what else they knew so I brought everybody out here to the other house," Ky-mani said, walking past and unlocking the car.

He pulled open the passenger door but I opened the back passenger door and climbed in instead. He laughed and shut back the door he opened.

Momma Doreen climbed in next to me and laughed.

When we arrived, I was in shock. It wasn't a house so to speak, it was a huge villa, the kind that families vacated in. It was a ten bedroom, eleven and a half bathrooms, waterfront, nine thousand square feet estate sitting on seventy- four acres. It was white and glass with an outdoor pool. It looked so beautiful at night surrounded by palm trees.

"Wow," I said. I've seen properties in my lifetime but never anything as beautiful as this.

When we walked in, the first thing I noticed was small kids' shoes, so I knew Chyna and Mani were there, and that also meant Monae too.

I had not seen her since she posted all that shit on Facebook. I didn't know what I would do when I did but since some shit was going on in Chicago causing us all to be here, I would swallow my tongue just to keep the peace.

Momma Doreen asked if I was hungry but all I wanted to do was shower. "No, Momma, I'm ok just tired and want to have a shower," I said and she hugged me.

"Y'all room upstairs; Ky-mani will show you," she said, kissing my cheek.

"My room is upstairs; he can sleep somewhere else," I said, heading to the stairs.

"Like hell I am," he said, following me.

The room he led me to was decorated in white and gold finishing including the bathroom, so I knew it was Ky-mani's personal room. He dropped my bag and opened the closet. I couldn't believe it was packed with all my clothes and belongings from Chicago. I was only asleep for a whole day. When did he have time to do that?

"Thank you," I said and grabbed some clothes to put on after my shower. He grabbed some clothes too and a towel.

"I'mma shower across the hall," he said walking out.

I jumped in the shower and literally rubbed my skin raw. I knew that dude didn't rape me, but Ky-mani said he had his mouth on me and I wanted to rid him off of me.

Ky-mani was sitting on the bed when I walked back in. I had hoped he found another room to sleep in but no. But tomorrow I was going to find myself a spare room. Until he apologized for what he said, I wasn't going to forgive him or entertain his ass either.

He was going to learn the hard way that I wasn't like them other females.

I wasn't going to lie, he looked good topless in a pair of basketball shorts. He had definitely bulked up a little during that time I was hiding from him in the hotel but it seemed like he had done once again in these few weeks apart.

He had my head in the clouds just from one look. He was a fine ass nigga without a doubt but giving in to him would make it ok for him to talk to me the way he did and I wasn't going to be about that life. So, ignoring my pussy, I dropped my towel and creamed my skin. He sat and watched me like I was the damn TV but I ignored his ass. I pulled on my clothes and climbed in the bed.

"Ky-mani, are you not going to find somewhere else to sleep?" I asked as he climbed in the bed too.

As soon as I laid down, he rolled over on top of me and pinned my arms by my side.

"Honey, stop fucking with me, ma. And stop playing so damn hard to get," he said, leaning close to my face.

"That's your problem, you think I'm playing but I'm not," I said but he just stared down at me.

God, I wish we weren't fighting.

I thought as I looked at his sexy, thick lips. I just wanted to kiss them and suck on them.

101

"Get your ass off me, Ky-mani."

"Or what? We both know you ain't about to do shit," he said, looking at my lips.

"Look at your lips. So damn juicy and sexy. I should suck those things off your face," he said, licking his lips.

"Yeah go ahead and I will bite your ass," I said.

"Oh, you gonna bite me, Honey?" he asked and I let him know I wasn't playing. "I hear you, thug," he laughed at me.

"I got a good mind to slide this dick off in your ass Honey since you like to play about 'I ain't your woman, Ky-mani'," he said and as he did, I felt his dick harden against me.

He looked down at me and I could see the lustfulness in his eyes. If I wasn't so mad at him, I would probably allow whatever he was thinking but I wasn't about to spoil his ass. Even though his dick felt so good against my groin.

"Thank you for saving me, Ky-mani," I said in the sweetest voice. "But you better get your ass up off of me. You and your dick," I yelled and nudged his ass off.

"I wish your ass would try and fuck me," I said, rolling over onto my side with my back to him.

"Yeah don't be surprised if your ass wakes up screaming with my dick deep in your pussy," he said.

I shook my head and closed my eyes.

In the morning, I woke up to find Ky-mani hugged up behind me. His dick was hard and pressed against my ass. I tried to move but he held me in place and rubbed his hand down my thigh. "Get off, Ky-mani," I said and nudged him.

"Stop playing, ma, unless it's with my dick," he moaned, pressing it hard against my ass. "Damn you got it so hard it hurts," he moaned.

"Ky-mani, I'm not playing with you. Let me go."

"Yes, you are. You want this just as much as I do. You wanna know how I know?" He whispered and I nodded my head.

"Because of this," he said, grabbing a handful of my pussy.

"This fat pussy is hot and vibrating. Your ass

is just as horny as me. Stop playing and let me up in there," he groaned and grabbed my breast.

Before I could respond, I heard someone knocking on the door.

"Honey? Ky-mani? I made breakfast. Are y'all awake?" she asked outside the door.

Ky-mani put his hand over my mouth to keep me quiet but I knocked it down.

"Yeah, Momma Doreen we are awake. Come in!" I said smiling.

Ky-mani let me go and put some distance between our bodies but he grabbed my hand and rested it on his dick under the blanket.

Momma Doreen came in and opened our curtains.

"Ahhh, Momma. I was still trying to lie down," Ky-mani moaned.

"Nigga, please. You want some pussy. And if Honey wanted to give it to your ass, she wouldn't have called me in. Now bring your ass down for some breakfast and leave that girl alone," she said and backed out the room.

I laughed at Ky-mani and rolled out of the bed. He quickly rolled out after me and grabbed me. "I swear I'm gonna fuck your ass up, Honey. Giving me goddamn blue balls," he moaned, grabbing his dick.

"Let me go, boy," I pushed him and went off into the bathroom. That boy better leave my ass alone.

Lord help me!

Chapter Seven

Monae

I knew Law had money but oh my god, when I saw that villa I was in shock. I was mad at first when Ricky came banging on the door, demanding me and the kids go with him and especially when I saw Angel in his car already. But once I arrived, I was glad I came.

The kids and I were put in a room that was like a two-bed studio inside the house. Their room was all set up for them and I had a lovely king sized bed in my room. Thankfully, Angel was put on the other side of my wing, so I wasn't near her. I hated to see her pregnant by my man.

I wasn't sure what was going on but I wasn't complaining. I was finally somewhere where Law

106

laid his head at. His room was on a floor of its own like it was a separate apartment. I didn't see much of him the first morning but I didn't see bitch ass, Honey, either so I knew they were no longer together.

His family acknowledged me because of the kids but they didn't really fuck with me or Angel like that. But I didn't give a fuck, it wasn't their money or dick that I wanted. I just stayed my ass near Angel. I didn't hate her plus she was an important part in my sick games just in case little miss perfect did show up.

Ky-mani spent most of the day and night gone but he said until further notice, we all lived here so I knew I had the time to seduce him. Yeah I know, I was still after that dick but you couldn't blame a bitch like me for trying. Law had that magic stick that had my ass climbing the walls. I would never stop wanting it ever.

So, despite him being gone, I was quite happy to go to sleep and chase his ass tomorrow.

But I woke up to a goddamn nightmare. From my window, I could clearly see Law's wing. So, when I went to see if he was back, I saw him holding onto Honey's ass. Not only was she there but he had taken her ass up into his private section even though they weren't together! I watched as he tried his hardest to hold on to her but she pushed him off.

Whatever happened to them, he was sorry but she was on some good bullshit. Well since she was obviously done with him, the least I could do was help a bitch out. I was going to make her life misery until she completely left and never came back.

I hated that Momma Doreen referred to Honey as her daughter in law, even though they weren't even together. She never referred to me as that not even once. I blamed Ky-mani for that. She would have never known about me without Ky-mani running at the mouth laying all my shit bare. And she's hated me ever since. Her and his sisters accused my ass of trapping Ky-mani getting pregnant on purpose. Shit, they didn't know the truth they were just guessing.

When I came down for breakfast, Honey didn't even look my direction. That was the first time seeing her since my Facebook stunt and I expected cussing or even a beat down, but she kept her cool and ignored me. Damn even when I fucked her over she was a better woman.

I wanted her to wild out like a ratchet ass but

she didn't. I even kept staring at her just to get under her skin but I was completely invisible to her.

I hated the way my kids loved on her and her on them. They ran off right away to sit by her for breakfast. Ky-mani did them up a plate and they sat eating and looking up at her like she was something so treasured.

Ky-mani looked at her completely lovesick but she ignored him. I don't know what was happening with them but whatever it was, I just hoped it continued.

Ky-mani looked about done with his breakfast, so I got up and headed inside since Honey was entertaining the kids. I grabbed my towel and headed for the bathroom that was closest to Ky-mani's wing. I knew he would have to pass it when he headed to his room.

I kept the door opened and looked out for him. And sure enough, I saw him climbing the stairs. I quickly shut the door and pulled off my robe. I waited for a second before screaming at the top of my lungs.

And just like the gentleman I knew he was, I heard him banging on the door.

109

"Yo, who in there screaming like that?" I heard his sexy voice ask.

"It's me, Monae. Please help, Law," I yelled.

I heard him suck his teeth before turning the handle and walking in.

"Shit," he said, closing the door when he realized I was naked. "What are you playing at, Monae?" he asked annoyed.

"Nothing, Law. I was about to take a shower but my hair got caught somehow," I said, pointing to my hair tangled in the shower head.

Yes, I know what you were thinking. Did this trick just purposely snatch her hair on the fucking shower just to lure Law? I sure fucking did. Weave could be replaced but wasn't no nigga like Law.

He looked at me and shook his head. He approached me and reached above my head to unhook my hair.

Nigga smelt so good as I inhaled his magical scent. My mouth watered as his body pressed against mine. I closed my eyes and imagined his hands and mouth on me and his dick deep inside me. I was so in my thoughts that I didn't even notice that he loosened my hair and walked out until I heard the door close. I was butt ass naked and he didn't even look or touch me.

I was so angry. Any other nigga would have taken that shit but Ky-mani dismissed my ass like I wasn't shit to look at. I angrily pulled my clothes on and grabbed my shit. I was so mad that I stomped my feet to my room. Well, what I thought was my room; I was so mad that I busted into the wrong room.

My eyes bucked as I saw Honey standing there butt ass naked like the day she was born with Ky-mani down on his knees with one of her legs propped on his shoulders and his face buried deep in her pussy. This nigga was eating her pussy. But he never ate pussy! I was yet to meet a bitch whose pussy he did.

But there I was watching it for myself. She had him eating out her hand and pussy literally. His ass was French kissing the fuck out of her pussy, she couldn't even moan. That shit looked like it felt good. He had some motherfucking tongue skills without a doubt.

Her eyes were closed so she didn't see me standing there. Then Ky-mani stood and pulled his shorts down. I looked down and saw his huge dick standing like a motherfucking flag pole. Then her eyes met mine.

She screamed when she saw me and Ky-mani stood in front of her to hide her body. "Fuck, Monae!" he yelled at me, adjusting his dick back in his shorts. I immediately stepped out and slammed the door shut.

So, his ass walks into a room with me naked and doesn't even flinch but decides to go and find her instead. I couldn't even lie though her body was nice. Her titties were big and perky, her stomach was flat and her hips were spread as fuck. Her pussy was pretty with a groomed line of hair, yeah I looked! No wonder his ass overlooked me. Honey was perfect.

I knew she had a nice body that could clearly be seen in her clothes but she looked better naked if that was even possible? Me, I was the opposite. I was pretty and I had some ass and titties but they weren't big and perky like Honey's. I had a few stretch marks on my hips from the kids. And my waist wasn't so cut after having them nor was my stomach as flat as before them. I looked banging in clothes but naked I would definitely change a few things. But Honey?

Ohhh I hate that bitch!!!

I hated Killa so fucking much. He was the cause of all this shit. He just had to fuck up and make Honey leave his ass. Which then lead her to meet Law. At first, I tried to justify his actions and say that her pussy probably wasn't shit but Law had schooled my ass in that. Her pussy had to be on a different level for him to constantly want her ass no matter how many times I threw mine at him. And it damn sure was good enough for him to sample with his mouth.

I needed to know. Surely Honey couldn't have him wide open like that? He never fucked me raw but he did Angel, so it was nothing to see him about to shove his dick in her raw like that. But eating pussy?
There was only one other person I knew that he fucked recently and that was Angel. I needed to know that it wasn't a Honey only thing. I had to know. Please God!

I made my way to Angel's room. I knocked and waited until she told me to come before I walked in. I had seen enough of Law's women naked for one day.
"What's up, Monae? Before you say anything, I know Law's woman is here," she said, rolling her eyes.

As I looked at her I wondered why Law started fucking her. She was very pretty, she looked a little like Kerry Washington but she was short and dark skinned, and a little thicker compared to me and Honey. I thought his type was slim thick, a little taller and fairer in complexion. Honey was a little more chocolate compared to me and Angel was dark chocolate. Maybe he didn't have a type.

"She's not his woman anymore. I heard her tell him that herself. Something is going on with them," I said but she just rolled her eyes again.

"Listen, maybe someone should tell his ass that because all he seems to do is follow her ass around. Why you think I grabbed some food and came right up here?" she said.

"Yeah well, that's what I heard. But let me ask you something," I said and she nodded her head and continued faffing about with her iPad.

"Did Law ever eat your pussy?" I whispered.

This bitch looked at me and started laughing her ass off like I asked her a joke or something.

"Bitch, why you laughing?" I asked with my hands on my hips. Did she not realize that I was asking her an important fucking question?

114

"Because that was a fucking funny question. Law eat my pussy? I wished! He made it clear he ain't trusting no bitch to kiss or eat their pussy. He never once did to me or anybody else I knew he fucked. The only girl he ever did it to was when he was a teen and before Law. But since he's been on the streets, his lips ain't touched a bitch's lips or pussy. Well except Honey's lips that is. When I saw him kiss her at his birthday party I couldn't believe it," she said, shaking her head.

"Why did you ask, Monae?" she asked raising an eyebrow at me. I couldn't tell her what I just saw. I could see in her face that she was weak, so if I revealed that, her ass would definitely bow out from helping me destroy their relationship. The fact he's never sucked on a pussy in years but did to her speaks volumes.

She was it for him. She was going to be the last woman who he would ever be with. If she was just a means for him to start wanting to eat pussy again, he would have tried one or two people by now. But he did it on her ass because he knew she would be the only one.

"I just wondered that's all," I lied.

"So Angel just between you and me, since he's met Honey have you fucked him again?" I asked and she looked at me.

"Honestly no. I ain't fucked him since I got pregnant before he met her. Why have you?" she said and I had to think before I answered. My mouth wanted to say yes but I shook my head no instead.

"Yeah I can believe that I've seen your Facebook post," she said laughing. Yeah, that shit was still up even until now. He was adamant he would beat my ass if I took it down and I didn't want to see if that was true.

He made me stink even more than I did with that post. It was bad enough that people called me the bitch who cried wolf but now they were calling me lying pussy bitch. If he was looking to destroy me then he accomplished that!

I didn't feel like talking anymore, so I left Angel and headed back to my room. But before I could even get there, I was yoked back by Law. He pushed me hard into the wall and pinned me down by my throat.

"You did that shit on purpose! Couldn't handle the fact I turned your ass down, so you deliberately came into her room to fuck up my nut, right? If you can't have the dick; then no one can huh, Monae?" he growled.

I take it from his action that after seeing me, Honey no longer wanted to fuck.

"Oh please, how was I supposed to know that was her room?"

"Yeah but you didn't walk your ass out right away did you?"

"Do you think I wanted to see you fuck her or suck on her pussy?" I threw back.

A wicked grin crept across his face and at that point I knew he was glad I saw that.

"What can I say? My baby tastes like fruit," he smiled and licked his lips.

"Oh and good try today," he breathed hard mimicking me before walking away laughing.

Shit, I didn't even realize I was breathing like that. But you don't know the powers that he had. I almost busted a nut just from him standing in front of me.

That trifling bitch. They weren't together but she still allowed him to sample the pussy.

Oooh, I hate the bitch!!!

Chapter Eight

Law

Honey was still walking around ignoring me. I didn't know what else to say or do. She wasn't even allowing me to fuck her!

The first morning she made my momma walk in so I couldn't do shit. But after breakfast, I caught her ass as she went into her room to change. Yeah, she moved into another room right after breakfast! Ma was straight tripping.

But in my haste to get to her, I forgot to lock back the door and Monae caught my ass trying to fuck. I was glad her ass caught me after that stupid stunt she pulled catching her own hair in the fucking shower. But when Honey no longer wanted to fuck, I was mad as hell. It had been too long since Honey sat on my dick and it was missing home!

To go from daily fucking and I meant daily. I

119

was straight breaking ma's back out every day from that first night. Unless she had her cycle, we were fucking and multiple times too.

So, to go from that to days of nothing was killing a nigga. Other than a quick taste of her pussy that one time, my ass was getting nothing.

"I love this place but I wish I could leave even just once!" Toya moaned to Honey and Nevaeh as they gossiped by the pool.

"I miss my friends and clubbing," she said.

"Yeah me too. The sooner we can go home the better," Nevaeh chimed in.

"I understand how you two feel," Honey said as they got up to get some sodas.

"I miss my girls so much. I can't wait to see them and party my ass off too," she smiled.

"When I get my new apartment, y'all should come over for one of our ladies' night and maybe we can hit up a club," she said and my sisters smiled and agreed.

They walked past my ass and I just stared at Honey. She was fucking me up with all this damn apartment talk.

But when she made a comment about liking being single, I had enough. I jumped to my feet and approached her.

"Honey, let me holler at you for a minute," I said but she kept on walking.

"No," she said and I shook my head.

"Yo, Honey, for real stop playing with my ass!" I yelled after her.

"Yo, Unc, are you not going to say sumthing?" I turned to him.

"Hell no, nephew, that's your woman," he laughed.

"I'm not his woman!" she yelled behind me, making everybody laugh including Angel and Monae

.

"For real, ma, I'm about to break my foot off in your ass!" I said and she rolled her eyes at me.

I sat down at the table and watched Honey as she talked and laughed with my sisters.

Why the fuck was this happening? Things weren't supposed to be that way, my baby and I shouldn't have been that way. But yet there we were and in front of those smug bitches. Monae was fucking me off with her smirks whenever Honey shut my ass down. And Angel was forever asking dumb ass questions about 'us'.

Bitch there was no us nor will there ever be. I needed and wanted my baby back.

I looked back around to Honey but she wasn't sitting where she was, in my thoughts, I didn't even notice that she had walked back into the house. Everybody was out in the garden by the pool, so that left the house empty.

"Momma keep everyone outside for me until I get back please," I whispered over to her. She looked at me and smirked.

"Handle your business, nephew," my Unc laughed and winked.

"Perv," My momma said, laughing and nodding her head.

I didn't care who did see me and who didn't. I jumped up to my feet and dashed in the house after Honey. She was on her way out when I walked in.

She looked at me and went to step around me but I blocked her path.

"Yo, ma, when you gonna cut all this bullshit out? I've apologized a thousand times!" I said.

"And you can apologize for a thousand more. But until you apologize for the right thing, I'm sorry for everything don't cut it for me," she said.

"Ma, stop playing with my ass. I think I definitely need to break this dick off in you to make you come to your senses."

"I am but like I told you, you obviously don't realize who you're dealing with. I ain't no common ass hoe, so I'm sorry for everything and slinging dick ain't gone change shit," she said.

"Yeah we'll see about that!" I said.

She went to run but I grabbed her ass and threw her over my shoulder.

"Put me down, Ky-mani!" she screamed and I smacked her ass.

"Oh, I'mma put you down…on this dick," I said, carrying her to the stairs.

As we passed the doorway, she screamed out.

"Momma Doreen, tell Ky-mani to put me down!" she screamed.

"What did you say, baby? I didn't hear you," my Ma said and I laughed.

"Marco!" she yelled.

"What you say, baby girl? I can't hear you," he

said and my family all started laughing.

I pulled her ass up the stairs and I felt her fold her arms across her chest despite hanging over my shoulder.

"About time your ass got with the program."

"You really think your ass is about to change something?" she said and I chuckled.

"We'll see how your ass feels once I'm up in them guts," I said, smacking her ass again.

I dropped her down on the bed in my room before going back to lock the door. I definitely didn't wantanyone to interrupt this.

I immediately started taking off my clothes and she laughed.

"Ky-mani, you better chill," she laughed when I pulled at her tee shirt.

"Ma, don't stop me," I said, looking her dead in her eyes. After a few seconds, she lifted her arms up and allowed me to pull it off. I pushed her down and pulled the strings on her bikini bottoms making it pop off.

I instantly dropped my mouth on her pussy. I craved her hypnotic fruity taste.

"Ahhh," she groaned and sucked on my middle

finger. I was so horny my dick was hurting. I could finish tasting her later but for now, my dick hungered for her. I climbed up the bed, pulling the strings on her top and released her breasts. I grabbed them and sucked hard on them before slipping my tongue into her mouth and my dick up in her guts.

As soon as my dick hit her pussy, I paused. It had been a minute since I felt my baby and she felt better than I remembered. I instantly pulled my dick out and looked down. She had my ass ready to nut just from sliding in.

"Goddamn, Honey," I said, smiling and rubbing my dick.

"Is something wrong?" she panicked and I smiled.

"Nah, baby, everything is all right," I said, sliding back in her warmth.

"Oh fuck, baby. I love you so much," I groaned and thrusted in and out long and deep to the end of my dick.

"You still love me?" I asked her as I stroked her insides. "Honey?" I said.

"Mmm, Ky-mani," she purred.

"Ma, do you still love me?" I said again.

"Yes, Ky-mani, I do. I do love you, daddy," she

said and my ass went wild.

"Shit ma, baby, you got me wide open," I grunted and kissed her. She moaned in my mouth.

I pushed back onto my knees, lifted her legs on my shoulders and thrusted deep inside.

"Fuck me, Honey, what you been doing to my pussy?" I growled. That shit was tight as fuck and wet, throbbing around my dick.

"That's it, baby…pop my pussy on me," I said as she rotated her hips with every move.

"This still my pussy, right?" I asked.

"Yes, Ky-mani, yes baby it is," she groaned.

"You sure, Honey? This is still my pussy, baby?" I said and she nodded biting down on her lips.

My ass started to shake and I gripped her hips tight fucking her rapidly.

"Oh fuck," I shook and closed my eyes.

"Ahhhh! Ky-mani. Shit, shit, shhhiiitttt!" she groaned, shaking as she came all over my dick.

I dropped my lips to hers and my ass started to buck. I pushed my dick deep one last time, before pulling out and busting in my hand.

"Ahhhhh fuck!" I growled and shook my head.

I staggered to my feet and wobbled into my bathroom. My legs felt like jelly. Ma almost tapped me out but I wasn't done just yet. I cleaned myself up and grabbed a washcloth for Honey. She was lying on her side in a ball and I laughed.

"You trying to kill my ass," she chuckled as I turned her over.

I gently cleaned her up with the damp cloth. I dropped it on the side table and turned my attention back to her pussy.

I rubbed my finger against it and she shuddered. I dropped my head down and circled my tongue on her clit. I sucked it into my mouth like a straw and nibbled on it before releasing it again. I sucked it back into my mouth sucking hard again before releasing it once more.

"Damn, Ky-mani," she hissed as I did that over and over again. As her moans intensified, so did my licking and sucking.

I sucked two fingers and slid them inside her. I

stroked her gently with them and her walls vibrated against them.

I clamped on her clit and sucked until she screamed out and came against my lips.

As she was still shaking, I pushed my dick inside.

"Sssss," she hissed and arched her back.

"Damn, Honey, you got the motherfucking best pussy ever, I ain't even lying," I whispered.

Ma had that killer pussy that I just wanted to live in. If I could walk around with my dick permanently up in there I motherfucking would.

I flipped her ass over and sat on her booty. I pulled her ass cheeks apart and slid my dick into her wet pussy.

"Fuck," I spat and smacked her ass. That shit jingled so I smacked it again. I grabbed two big handfuls of her ass and held on to steady myself as I fucked the shit out of her.

She sunk her face in the pillows as she screamed busting a big nut.

The shit felt so good that I didn't even get a chance to pull out; I busted my seeds deep up in her pussy.

"Shit, ma, sorry," I panted.

I rolled off the bed to clean myself up.

When I looked over at Honey, she was laying on her side, eyes closed with a hand between her thighs. I knocked her ass out. I laughed and pulled the blanket up over her.

I pulled my clothes on and went downstairs feeling like the boss nigga that I am.

"Ky-mani, what your ass do to my daughter-in-law?" My momma asked as I slumped in a chair.

"Nothing, Momma, she asleep," I smiled and my Unc dapped me up.

"Oh, you slung it on her ass good," we both laughed.

My momma and aunt looked at us and shook their heads.

I really did sling that dick well on Honey because a few hours later, she still hadn't come back downstairs.

"Yo, Law, you fucked her ass up good," my uncle laughed and my momma smacked him.

"Ky-mani, go up them stairs and go feed my

129

baby. You wrong for tapping her out like that," she said and I laughed.

I took the food that she handed me and stood to my feet. "Ok, Ma," I laughed.

Monae and Angel sat staring at my ass. I knew they heard what my momma said and I didn't give a fuck. I grabbed my dick and smirked letting them know exactly what my ass did to Honey. I grabbed my drink and walked away.

When I got into my room, Honey was just sitting up.

"Wow, Ma, I fucked you up that good?" I said, laughing and she rolled her eyes at me.

"Shut up fool," she laughed. "I don't know, I'm just so tired," she stretched.

"I brought you something to eat," I said, setting the plate of food beside her.

"Hmmm thank you," she smiled and jumped up going into the bathroom.

I followed her and watched her peach ass jiggle with every step. She brushed her teeth and jumped in the shower. I could watch her all day.

I leaned against the door frame and enjoyed the show. She hopped out and smiled at me as she passed.

She dried her body off, put lotion on her skin, and pulled on one of my t-shirts.

"Mmm," she said as she tucked into the plate.

"Greedy ass," I laughed and she stuck her tongue out at me. I left her eating and went for a shower.

When I came out, the plate was clean and she was sat up in bed with a satisfied smirk on her face.

"Damn, ma, you ate all that food?" I laughed and she nodded her head.

"Damn right. I had no energy left thanks to someone," she said, pointing at me.

I walked over to the bed and stood at her feet.

"So you all fed now, ma?" I asked and she nodded.

"Good," I said, dropping my towel. "Now feed me," I said, grabbing a foot and sliding her down to me.

She pulled off the tee and slipped off her panties. I dropped to my knees, feasted on her pussy, and fucked her ass back to sleep.

Chapter Nine

Killa

I had been every fucking where but I still couldn't find Honey or Monae. I saw Honey's friends but never her. She had changed her number; I got it from Monae but she never answered the call. I guess it wasn't a good idea to be calling her from the same number I have had for years. She probably recognized that shit.

I had been fucking Monae for a minute but it was just to get what I needed from her to get Honey back. We had planned for me to go into Law's house, using the code she gave me and fuck Honey sending pics to Law. But as the time for me to do it came and went, I knew something was wrong. I had planned the day when I would do it with Monae but Blacka decided he wanted me doing the goddamn shipment.

That nigga has never let me do it since his ass got here but the one night I planned to get at Honey, especially since Law was no longer in the house, this black motherfucker wanted me to now handle the shipments. I had watched Honey for three days and Law hadn't been around, so I just knew sooner or later he would. There was just no way he could stay away from her.

I was mad as fuck sitting at the docks waiting for the fucking shipment to get in. All I kept thinking was that I could have been balls deep in Honey's pussy like I used to. Blacka was fucking with my program.

But by the time I did the shipment and went the next night for Honey. The house was a goddamn pile of ashes and she was gone, along with Law, Monae, and his whole fucking crew. My one shot at fucking with Law and getting Honey back was gone.

Blacka was by the office, so I headed over there to see if he had any plans on finding Law. Because finding him would be finding Honey. I came into the building and as I climbed the stairs, I could hear him in a heated argument.

"Yo, Don, that's not my fucking fault that Law caught that nigga. All he had to do was go in there and fuck Law's woman and get the fuck out. I provided the fucking code so I did my part," he yelled.

"No, I don't know where the fuck he be at! Shouldn't your ass know that shit?!" He paced the floor.

"Nigga, what the fuck you mean? You can't cut my ass out, I put my motherfucking money up not your ass. If we just stuck to the original plan, we would have had his ass by now. You're the one who jumped the gun and tried to have some young niggas grab his ass," Blacka said.

"Oh for real, nigga, that's how you feel? After two years of planning and all my hard-earned cash, you wanna go solo? So, what about my six mils; am I gonna get that back?" I could see in his eyes that he was scared.

"Wow, my nigga, that's how you really feel? No problem but I'm shutting this fucking club down and taking my ass home. Fuck this," he spat before hanging up.

"You can come out now, Killa," he said with his back to me.

"Yo, Blacka, what the fuck was all that about?"

"My nigga stop acting like a fucking female

wanting to know shit and asking questions," he flapped his hand at me.

"Nah rid me of that shit, Cuz, and tell me what's good," I said.

"Oh, it's like that huh, braveheart?" He laughed. "Ok then. I sent a nigga from outta town to Law's crib to fuck his woman. But somehow Law found out and murked the nigga. He took his family and disappeared. And no one knows where he at," he said so blankly.

"Motherfucker, didn't I tell your ass that she was my woman?! You sent a random nigga to rape my girl?" I flipped out and approached him. Sure, I was planning on doing the same thing but she knew me and was with me before, so it wouldn't have been rape.

She knew this dick; it wasn't foreign to her. But Blacka sending someone in to do what I was supposed to do let me know Monae fucked me over.

As I stepped up to his ass, he grabbed me and put his gun under my chin.

"Motherfucker, you wanna do something?" he said and I just stared his ass down.

"You fucked me, Blacka. And that's why your ass

135

sent me to the docks. So, you could have somebody else rape Honey."

"Nigga, please, your ass was going to do the same thing anyway," he shrugged his shoulders.

"That ain't even the same thing. She's tasted this dick before," I let him know.

"So how did you find out?" I asked and he dropped the gun by his side.

"Cuz, you really believe Monae was only sitting on your dick?" he laughed.

"It's done now so forget about it. I need your mind right because tomorrow we shutting this motherfucking club down. The Don thinks he can just cut my ass out? Hell fucking no," he said, grabbing his phone.

"Meet me downstairs at the car when you done bitching. But remember this, if I had let your ass go, it would have been your bones in that motherfucking ash," he said before stepping out.

I knew Monae's ass was a hoe from the jump, so I'm not surprised that she was fucking Blacka too and she couldn't understand why Law wanted my girl? Why the fuck would he want a loose pussy hoe when he could have a Queen like Honey?

But what got to me was that she was so hell bent on getting rid of Honey that she felt no way having a complete stranger go into the house and fuck her!

No wonder Law ended his life, I wanted to and I didn't know him. But I knew that Blacka caused this. Cousin or not, he had a random dick nigga fuck my girl! This motherfucker needed to die for that. I did Honey so wrong but killing Blacka would be a right for Honey.

I opened the safe and grabbed a gun. I locked it back up and tucked the gun behind me. I turned the light out and went down to Blacka.

His car was running as he sat waiting for me. I looked around to make sure nobody else was around. I pulled my gun from my back and held it down so he wouldn't see it. I braced myself and yanked open the door raising my gun at the same time.

What the fuck? I thought as Blacka was leaning over onto the window dead with blood and shit oozing from a huge hole in his head.

"I beat you to it, my nigga," I heard behind me

and I turned to see the same guy he was fucking with before, standing there with a gun pointed at me.

What the hell was going on? I never knew this nigga's name but I knew Blacka trusted him and now he killed him?

"What the fuck? Aren't you his boy?" I asked the nigga.

"I was never his boy! I was just using the fat motherfucker to get to Law. But he wasn't no fucking help," he said smirking. He still had his gun pointed at me.

"I see you were about to do him yourself, so I guess we're not so different after all," he said.

"So what now; you gone kill me too?"

"That depends on what you wanna do? You can stay here and die or you can fuck off somewhere. I see you're not for these streets so I can't even fuck with you like that. But I know your ass ain't gone say nothing as you were about to do the same got damn thing," he nodded his head towards the gun in my hand.

I slowly put the gun in my back and put my hands out. He smirked, put his away, and walked away. I watched until he disappeared into the club before I turned back to Blacka. I grabbed his watch, cell phone, and wallet; fuck it he didn't need it anymore!

I jumped in my car and sped to my crib. I needed to get my shit and leave this fucking state. I called Dog and told him to get the fuck out and meet me in Minnesota; I had people out there I knew so I would be OK to hide out there for some time until I found Honey.

As I pulled into my driveway, I was shocked to see my front door wide open and different men going in and out. A tall, white man knocked my window and told me to get out the car with my hands up. Fuck, Police!

I opened my door slowly and climbed out. He grabbed me, slammed me down on the hood of my car, and handcuffed me.

He led me into my house and sat me down on my couch, as the other cops searched my house.

"Ayo, what the fuck you arresting me fo'?" I spat.

"For attempted murder and the unlawful abortion

139

of a fetus," a short black cop said to me.

"Come again?" I asked.

"For trying to kill me!" I heard and I looked up to see Trixie. My eyes popped out of my head. The bitch was still alive!!!

She walked over to the officer and whispered something to him. He looked at me and smirked before walking away.

Trixie came over and slapped me across the face.

"Nigga, I loved you and you tried to kill me for that bitch who doesn't even want your ass! You are a stupid nigga anyway; you don't know how to feel for a pulse?" she laughed.

"Trixie, baby, I can explain. I was losing my mind at the time, I wasn't thinking. I'm sorry, baby," I pleaded.

"Nah, nigga, fuck that. I lost my baby because of you. You're gonna pay for what you did," she looked at me and smiled. Just then the officers came back into the room. They were confiscating all my shit, even the sixty thousand dollars I had in my safe. The officer grabbed me and pulled me up to my feet.

Trixie came over and whispered in my ear.

"I set Honey's house on fire; I was hoping to kill the bitch. But don't worry, when my new man, The Don, finds Law, I promise to make your bitch die a slow painful death. Enjoy prison with your pretty ass. Don't drop the soap," she looked at me and then kissed my cheek.

"Trixie, bitch, don't you dare! Fuck you, bitch; I wished I killed your ass, bitch. If you touch even a hair on my baby's head, you will regret it! Do you HEAR ME YOU, BITCH? YOU WHORE!!!" I yelled as they dragged my ass out of my house.

Protect my girl, Law; she's yours now. I'm sorry, Honey. I thought and prayed as I was driven away.

Chapter Ten
Honey

Three weeks had passed and we were still here and I wished I wasn't. I missed my girls so freaking much. Because Ky-mani didn't know who was after us, we weren't allowed to make contact with them at all. He sent messages to them from the guys on burner phones but other than that I had no direct contact with them.

I was so damn miserable it was unreal.

Man, I wished I was home and not here anymore. Somebody just had to break into our house and try to get at me, didn't they? I still didn't know how Ky-mani came to find out or what he was doing over there in the first place. But being there with those bitches made me wish he hadn't.

They were so pathetic, making comments whenever I passed and I wanted to beat their asses so badly but I just couldn't with Ky-mani's family there.

I didn't want to cause any drama in their home but it was getting harder and harder to let shit slide.

And then on top of that, Ky-mani was harassing my ass about forgiving him and being back together. As much as I wanted to, I just couldn't.

He said some things to me that he just shouldn't have and I just needed to hear him apologize for it but he was so stuck on apologizing for everything with his stubborn ass and it just was not the same for me.

Maybe I shouldn't have fucked him but the love was there and the attraction was real, it was so hard to stay away. But I tried to show him that it wouldn't change because I knew myself and knew that it was something I couldn't let go.

But he couldn't understand that; we fucked so all should be good. But me telling him no made things a whole lot worse. He was on a rampage and everybody in his path was getting it and I was no exception.

"Ky-mani, why is your face like that?" Aunt Ruth asked him as he sat mean mugging my ass.

"Because, Aunt, some people think I'm a fucking joke. But when I beat her ass she will know what time it is," he threw his words at me.

"Go ahead, Ky-mani, and I bet I'mma hit your ass right back. You wanna sit there with a damn attitude, fine, but don't for a second think I'm just gonna let you beat my ass," I looked at him.

Clearly, I was no match for Ky-mani and he knew that too. But doesn't mean I was just going to take the beat down without even trying to fight back. I may not do any damage but I damn sure was going to try.

"Honey, stop fucking with me, ma! I keep warning your ass," he said but I just ignored him.

"You better come to your damn senses right the fuck now. And go get your shit and bring your ass back to my room. I'm done fucking sleeping in separate rooms to my woman, so get with the motherfucking program and stop all this goddamn bullshit!"

"Ky-mani, you and I both know what's going on here and that I'm not your woman," I said, knocking him down. I got up and walked away and he was hot on my tail.

"Whatever, Honey, you already know what time

it is. I wrote my name all in that pussy and you know that shit," he said, grabbing his dick.

"I guess it's time I changed the author," I said and his smile instantly disappeared. I chuckled and continued walking inside.

"Yo, ma, for real stop. You like to play games too much, Honey," he said, grabbing my arm pulling me back to him.

"What games, Ky-mani? I told your ass it wouldn't change shit but you still did it like my ass was joking. But now you played yourself and you mad at me," I said.

"The fuck you mean? You weren't saying all that shit when you were taking the dick, Honey," he said angrily.

"Ky-mani, that's sex talk," I said and he shook his head at me.

"I told you before, Ky-mani, you ain't dealing with a stupid, uneducated bitch that you can just fuck and make everything ok. Just like I know I ain't dealing with no regular nigga, you need to know I ain't no regular female. I'm not the one who needs to get to their senses. I ain't playing games; I'm waiting on your ass to clue up, Ky-mani," I said and walked away.

145

I went up and grabbed my bathing suit to go swim with the kids. He didn't say a damn word to me when I went back out to the poolside. I just took the kids by the hands and pulled them into the pool with me.

After some time, I was done swimming.

"Y'all go get some ice cream from grandma," I said to the kids as we climbed out of the pool.

I was surprised when they both hugged me and then ran off. I looked up to see Monae rolling her eyes at me. I shook my head and picked up my towel.

Ky-mani watched me as I passed but I turned my head. He could be as mad as he wanted. I told him that him slinging dick wasn't going to change shit.

I went into my room laid out some clothes and went into the family sized bathroom in the hall for a shower.

I washed my hair as well in the shower. I stepped out and pulled my hair up into a tight bun. I dried my skin and put my robe on. I collected my items and opened the door to leave.

When I did, Ky-mani came pushing me back

inside and locked the door.

He picked me up and sat me on the countertop and rested his body between my legs. He dropped his head on mine and closed his eyes.

"Ma, I'm going out of my mind. Don't you love me anymore?" he asked and sighed.

"I do, Ky-mani," I said because honestly, I did. But I needed him to know he couldn't just do and say as he pleased with me. I knew my boundaries and limits with him but if he did, there's no way he would have said what he did that night. And me rolling over would be saying it was ok and it wasn't. He hurt me deep with his comments and he needed to understand that so he wouldn't do it again.

"So if you still love me, please, ma, tell me what I did so I can fix it," he said looking me in the eyes.

"I can't, Ky-mani. I need you to do it yourself," I said and he stroked my face and ran his thumb along my bottom lip.

He kissed me and tried to pull my robe open but I stopped him. "Ky-mani, this isn't going to help," I shook my head.

"It's ok, ma, I know it won't change anything

147

but just let me please," he whispered, kissing me again.

He slipped his tongue into my mouth and opened my robe. He licked down my neck and sucked on my breasts. He licked further down until he reached my pussy. He licked and sucked on my pussy lips and clit before dipping his tongue in and out of me. He sucked every angle of my pussy before standing up to his feet and dropping his basketball shorts. He grabbed his dick and gently entered me.

"I love you, Honey," he moaned before attacking my lips with his.

He grabbed my hips in his hands and thrusted hard and fast. My body was thumping up against the wall and mirror, making all kinds of shit fall to the ground but it felt too good to stop.

Someone came knocking on the door but Ky-mani continued. "Ky-mani, someone is at the door," I said but he continued.

"Ahhh shit. Fuck them, there's eleven bathrooms in this bitch," he grunted and kissed me again.

He continued knocking my back out with somebody still beating on the door.

"Yo, I'm in here. Wait a minute!" he shouted.

"Damn niggas fucking up my nut," he moaned and I laughed.

We kissed each other deeply again and he squeezed my ass. I moaned into his mouth as I came, shaking my legs and tapping my hands on the side. He dropped his head in my neck and started pounding into my pussy making my moans back up in my throat.

"Shit!" he said as he got faster and faster until he nutted. "Fuck me!" he said pulling out and dropping his head on my shoulder.

We looked at each other and laughed. I handed him a wash cloth and I jumped back in the shower to clean myself up quickly. He handed me my towel when I stepped out and dried me off. I pulled on my robe and we made sure the bathroom was right before pulling the door open.

Monae was standing outside with her arms folded. Ky-mani smiled at her. "All yours, ma," he said and grabbed me by the hand and pulled me down the hall with him.

If I was a petty bitch I would have screamed out louder if I knew it was her out there. I was yet to

149

address her for the shit she pulled on Facebook but I figured her hearing me fuck Ky-mani was punishment enough.

***

Being locked up in this house altogether was starting to take its toll on me. I turned one direction and I was faced with Ky-mani and his questions and I turned the other and was faced with Monae and Angel's stink asses.

I was so caught up in the moment that I allowed Ky-mani to fuck me like that in the bathroom.

Monae made a smart-ass comment as I passed, about me not being any different than them and in a respect, she was right. I should have known better. But at the same time, he should have never rushed his ass into the bathroom like that. I felt dirty like I had fucked him in a club bathroom or something.

Ky-mani tried to say something to me but I brushed him off. So, he grabbed me and yanked me into the kitchen with him.

"What the fuck is your problem?" he asked.

"You, Ky-mani. You got me looking like a damn thot to your baby mommas fucking me like that in the bathroom. I feel so ashamed that I allowed you to get me caught up," I said. He pushed me up into the refrigerator and leaned his body against mine.

"First of all, those bitches can't say shit to you because you are my goddamn wife and they know that shit. We are just going through something but that doesn't change and will not change the fact that I love your ass. Fuck what they think and the sooner you do too, we can get past this. Yes, I'm still the cause of this upset between us and I'm working on my shit but I know that some of this animosity that I feel from you is because of them."

"You are my motherfucking queen, Honey, and those bitches ain't shit compared to you. They wished a nigga would fuck them in a bathroom because compared to where they asses did get handled the motherfucking bathroom is a palace. Fuck what those unimportant bitches think, even if I fucked your ass all over this motherfucker, they still wouldn't be on your level because you got my heart, ma, so there's a huge

151

difference. I don't fuck you because I can, I do it because I'm in love with your ass and that's the closest I can be to you," he said, looking down into my eyes.

He ran his hand down my face stroking it gently. "I'mma leave you to think on that," he said, backing out the room.

"He's right you know," I heard and I jumped. I thought we were alone.

"Momma Doreen, I didn't know you were in here," I said, holding my chest from being scared shitless.

"I know. My ass was in the pantry minding your business as always," she cackled and I laughed.

"But you know he's right. Honey, me and his dad used to be tearing up the house, in the bathroom, the garage, the pool, and even in the car," she smiled, shaking her head as she went down memory lane.

"But never once did I feel like a hoe or thot to him even if I did it in places that a thot was known to do it in. There is a difference, Honey. It's not where you do it, it's who with!" she said, shaking a finger at me.

"So if a nigga fucks a hoe in a bed, she's not a

hoe? And if a husband fucks his wife in the bathroom, she a hoe? No way! It's who the sex is with that determines that difference. When a man loves a woman, he will make love to her everywhere and anywhere, it doesn't matter where as long as he's with her because he loves her, not because he's horny and wants some pussy. That's what he does with a hoe, Honey. You and Ky-mani are going through but I know that man loves you, Honey. You have his heart and no thot has a man's heart. You feel me, baby?" she said and I nodded my head. She pulled me into her arms and hugged me tight.

"Oh and like I been telling you, you need to put those bitches in their place, Honey. Shut those motherfuckers down. Don't be polite for me, baby, I've heard all kinds of shit my whole life, I ain't new to a good old fashioned cuss out. So, don't hold back for my ass if that's why you ain't said shit because I know you want to. Handle your shit baby and don't make me have to tell your ass again," she laughed and I smiled.

More people started pouring into the kitchen so she winked at me and ended the conversation. Ricky, Drake, and KY had finally arrived but Cameron was still in Atlanta.

"What up, sis?" Ricky said, hugging me.

"How are you doing?"

"I'm doing good, Ricky, and you?"

"Yep, shit I'm glad to be here. Yo' man had me working my ass off," he laughed and I smiled.

Monae walked passed and scoffed at Ricky calling Ky-mani my man but I ignored her.

"Yo, sis, let a nigga know if I have to air some motherfuckers out for you. You know how my finger stays wanting to pump," he said, making trigger pulling moves in the air. I laughed and shook my head.

"Nah I'm good thanks," I smiled and hugged him. KY and Drake came over and hugged me too.

We all sat outside to eat. We laughed and joked about everything. My girls were definitely missing but they had their lives to live so I couldn't expect them to give it up and come out here.

It wasn't even late and my ass was tired. The exhaustion was making me feel sick and gave me a headache. Maybe a few aspirin and some sleep would help, so I decided to go up to my room.

154

When I woke up in the morning, my head was spinning and I felt sick as fuck. I rolled out of the bed and went into the bathroom across the hall. By the time I locked the door, I vomited bucket loads into the toilet. I slumped on the floor and the cold tiles felt good. I stayed in the bathroom for a while vomiting a few more times, before I brushed my teeth and went back to my room.

After I had my shower, I didn't feel any better but I thought maybe food would help. When I went down everybody was up eating breakfast, so I went to fix me up a plate. I loaded my plate with mainly junk food, which was so unlike me but it was what I wanted.

"The fuck you eating all that junk food for?" Ky-mani barked at me.

"Leave me alone, Ky-mani, I'm missing my girls and my momma," I said, flapping my hand at him. I didn't wanna be bothered, so I took my plate back up to my room.

A few hours later and I found myself in the bathroom again vomiting. I was stressing myself to the point of sickness...well, I hoped it was that!

155

There was a medical supply room on the ground floor, I made my way there to grab something important. Luckily they had one, so I stashed it in my purse and made my way back up to my floor but Ky-mani found me.

I put my head down and tried to walk around him but he grabbed me and backed me up into the wall.

"What is your problem, ma?"

"Ky-mani, I am not your thot," I snapped at him.

He closed his eyes and pinched the bridge of his nose.

"We are not together, Ky-mani, you walked out. So, we have no business fucking like we are. But you seem to think I'm your personal hoe and I'm not. Don't treat me like them."

"First of all, I have never ever treated you like a thot Honey. I can't help that I love your ass why I keep wanting to stick my dick you in. But I guess love don't live in your heart for me anymore. You talk about you ain't my thot but I've done nothing but treat your ass like the Queen you are but that's not good enough. At least those thots know what the fuck they want," he said in my face.

"Well leave me the hell alone then and go be with one of those thots," I said.

He looked me up and down and shook his head at me.

He took a step back from me and pointed his right arm towards the step. "Walk away Honey," he said and I did.

I rushed up to the bathroom and locked the door. I pulled the pregnancy test out of my purse and opened it. Yeah, I know! I couldn't be pregnant but something wasn't right with me.

I sat on the toilet and reluctantly peed on the stick. I set the cover back on and sat it down on the counter on top of some paper towel. I remained on the toilet for five minutes just staring into space. My eyes fell on the test and after fixing back my clothes and flushing, I approached it.

I turned it over and there as clear as day were two fucking lines...my ass was pregnant!

I could do nothing but drop on the edge of the

bathtub and cry my fucking eyes out. I cried until my chest started to hurt. I couldn't be pregnant; I didn't want to be pregnant.

When I was all cried out, I wrapped up the test and packaging and placed them in my purse so I could dispose of them later. I dried my eyes and left the bathroom.

As soon I did, I bumped smack into Aunt Ruth. She looked me up and down before taking me by the hand and leading me to her bedroom.

"What's going on, baby girl?" she asked, eyeing me.

"I'm just missing my family and friends," I sniffled.

"Yeah I believe that but there's more to it. What's going on?" she asked but I stayed quiet.

"You can talk to me, baby, I ain't gon tell nobody," she smiled. I looked around the room before making eye contact with her.

"I'm pregnant, Aunt Ruth," I finally admitted and she hugged me.

"Oh, baby, it's gon' be alright. Have you told Ky-mani?" she asked and I shook my head.

158

"I'm too scared to," I admitted.

"You should tell him."

"I know Aunt Ruth but this is not what I wanted. He's already got a baby coming and I didn't want anyone to think I did this because of Angel or because I am trying to trap him or anything like that. So much has happened between us so I know that's how it looks," I said, wiping my tears.

"Baby girl, please. Even a blind man can see you and Ky-mani love each other. Fuck what people think; we, your family, know different. You ain't like them thots, Honey, you love him."

"Yeah I do but we are not exactly seeing eye to eye at the moment. I don't want him to pity me and want to get back together because I am."

"That is not going to happen. Can't you see that boy going crazy over you and he doesn't even know?"

"Talk to him, Honey, ok? But I won't say anything I promise," she said, hugging me.

She gave me some advice and I went back to my room.

What the fuck am I gone do now???

Could y'all tell him for me??

<u>Chapter Eleven</u>

Law

I sat at the table, rubbing my goatee thinking about Honey. I can't believe she accused me of thinking of her as my thot, yeah I know I was trying to lay major dick in her but not because of anything else other than I loved her.

Before it wasn't so difficult to be with her and we made love a few times but this last week, I could barely look at her let alone touch her. She was straight not allowing my ass.

All she was doing was moping around the house, sitting in silence, and eating mad junk food.

She was severely stressed and I couldn't even help. Even when I didn't want to fuck, which ok wasn't very often, she wouldn't even allow me to talk to her.

I ran my hand over my face and decided to go and try to talk to her again.

She spent a lot of time in her room, so I knew where she would be at.

161

I knocked on her door and waited for her to answer it. A few seconds later, she unlocked the door and pulled it open.

"Ky-mani?" she said, surprised to see me.

I gently pushed on the door and let myself in. I locked the door behind me and turned to face her.

Every step I made towards her, she took one back so I advanced towards her and backed her up to the wall.

I put up my hands against the wall and blocked her in. I leaned my body close to hers and looked into her beautiful eyes.

"Ma, you ready to talk to me?" I asked and she looked at me with worried eyes.

"By your face, I can see that you got something to tell me," I said and she continued to look up into my eyes.

"Ky-mani, I…," she started and then stopped.

"Tell me, Honey. Talk to me," I said, stroking her face gently.

"I'm pregnant, Ky-mani," she whispered.

My eyes damn near fell out of their sockets.

"Come again?" I asked her and she dropped

162

her head to the floor. I used my hand to lift her head back up and her face was filled with tears.

"I'm so sorry," she cried.

"How long have you known, Honey?"

"Since last week."

"Were you going to tell me?" I asked.

"Yes – I was just so scared," she sniffed.

"Of what, ma?" I stroked her face.

"I don't want people to think I'm a weak bitch and did this because I couldn't handle that Angel was or to trap you in any way. We've not been seeing eye to eye lately," she said and I closed my eyes.

"Honey, you are a Queen. You are far from a weak bitch. And you and I are like this because of me. And you're pregnant because I know my ass didn't pull out that night," I said, dropping my head.

"Damn, ma," I laughed and she slapped me.

"Sorry but I knew that ass was pregnant. That wasn't no normal pussy. Your stuff was hella wet," I continued to laugh.

I wasn't even lying, the first time I slipped back up in there; I had to pull my dick out before I nutted. My baby was tight and wet as fuck.

"Let me ask you something? Is that why this last week you've not allowed me to touch you?"

"Yes. I thought you would realize," she said and I started laughing.

Goddamn! Honey was pregnant!

I grabbed her and wrapped my arms around her. I pulled her head up and dropped my lips on hers. I claimed her lips and kissed her with all my love. She made a nigga happy she would never understand.

"So, ma, you having my baby?" I asked, smiling wide and stroking her face.

"I guess so," she laughed nervously. We looked at each other and laughed. I picked her up and spun her around. I rubbed my hand on her stomach and she placed her hand on top of mine.

"You know you're gonna have to marry me now, right?" I said serious as fuck but she rolled her eyes at me.

"Who told you I wanted to marry your ass anyway?" she laughed.

"Ma, I'm gonna make things right with us ok. And we are gonna be ok, the three of us," I said, kissing her and then her belly.

"I'mma hold you to that, Ky-mani."

"I love you, ma."

"I love you too, Ky-mani," she smiled. I kissed her one more time and laid her down to sleep.

I walked out that room feeling like a new man.

I walked out into the garden with a huge fucking grin onmy face.

"What the fuck you smiling at, nigga?" Drake said and everybody including Monae and Angel looked up at me.

"Ayo where the motherfucking Moët at? I'm about to celebrate up in this bitch. My goddamn baby is having my baby," I said.

"Honey is pregnant?!" Toya yelled clapping.

"Yes, she motherfucking is!" I danced.

My whole family got up and rushed me congratulating me.

"Motherfucker, go put that dick of yours in the dresser. Fucking walking around here dropping seeds like your black ass is a goddamn farmer," my momma said and we all laughed.

165

"How is she?" ma momma asked.

"She good, ma; she laughing and shit. I made her lay down for a while," I smiled.

"Goddamn, I'mma be a Papa bear," my Unc said and we all laughed at him.

I was so motherfucking happy my ass could have busted. My niggas opened a bottle of Moët and damn near drowned my ass in it, pouring it over my head. Then my sisters grabbed me and threw my ass in the pool. Fucking haters!

I didn't even dry my ass off; I didn't care about anything. My wife was having my baby! Can y'all believe it?

My Unc busted the sound system on and we started dancing our asses off. All except those bitches. I just smiled at them and continued dancing with my family. I didn't give a fuck about them.

I laughed when I imagined Killa flipping his lid finding this shit out.

Fuck me! I thought as shit finally hit my ass.

I knew what I did and I knew just how to make it better.

166

"Ma, I'mma do it tonight," I said and she kissed me.

I celebrated a little longer with my family before heading up to Honey but I took a quick detour to my safe and grabbed something. When I got into the room, she was awake looking washed out but still as beautiful as ever. My baby was definitely fucking her ass up but she looked happy.

Considering the argument, we had, about the whole pulling out situation, she was actually happy to be pregnant. This was a new chapter for us but I wanted to wipe the slate clean. I gave her a kiss and headed for a shower since I smelt like the pool and Moët.

I was nervous as hell during my shower, I was about to embark in the unknown with Honey. Yes, I had two kids already but if I'm honest I didn't pay Monae much mind until they were born. But this was going to be the first time I would experience pregnancy first hand and it gave me bubbles in my stomach.

I laughed my ass off. Honey was pregnant!!!

When I climbed out the shower, she was looking

so beautiful laying on top of the blanket in black lace panties and bra. Her skin was glowing and her eyes sparkled. This was the unknown for her too but I made a promise in my heart to be there with her every step of the way. Honey was it, my life, my happy beginning and ending. I could see nothing else but us and her being pregnant was like putting a ribbon on top but I was about to give her the bow.

"Honey," I said, pulling her up to sit on the bed with me kneeling down on the floor.

"Baby, I am so sorry I said what I did to you about Killa. When I said, I should go out there and cheat on you and get bitches pregnant. I am so sorry from the bottom of my heart; I should have never said something like that to you especially as it was a difficult time that you went through," I said and she sighed out of relief.

"I've been waiting for that. You hurt me so much by saying that, Ky-mani, because we both told each other things about our pasts but I would never use that as a weapon against you to hurt your feelings. But when you did, I was crushed," she said, crying and I wiped her tears away.

"We are in love, Ky-Mani, there are things we should never say to each other or do to hurt each other, whether we are angry or not. We are supposed to treat each other differently than we would someone on the streets. If I spoke to you how I would anybody else, then I can't love you or respect you," she said sniffling.

"You are right, ma, and if you forgive me I promise to never do that again," I wiped her tears.

"I have forgiven you, Ky-mani, from when the words left your mouth but I just needed you to see that it hurt me. But I need to take responsibility too because I know I pushed you. I'm sorry I was acting out about getting pregnant, I was just afraid, babe; I didn't want people to think I got pregnant to trap you or keep you. And I was looking for apartments because I didn't want us to change, Ky-mani."

"I have habits. I sleep wild, I leave my iPad around sometimes, I take a while to get dressed, I like everything to have a place, and I like things to match. I like having a girls' night once a month and we are crazy and wild, Ky-mani. I guess I'm just saying I didn't want my habits to get to you and you stop loving me. Because I love you so much I really do.

169

And I can't ever imagine loving anyone else," she said, looking me in my eyes.

"Ma, I been knowing your ass sleeps wild from that first night I stayed over," I chuckled and she laughed. "But on a real, all those other things you are worried about makes you who you are and I love everything about you. There's nothing you could do or say that would stop me from ever loving you Honey. I've never loved someone like I love you and I never will. As far as trapping, never Honey. Everybody knows a woman of your caliber could never do something like that. I know it's only been less than a year but does that mean that I can't be sure that I love you. You and I are made for each other and I will love you until the day I die," I said, reaching into my basketball shorts pocket that hung over the chair.

"Honey Unique Johnson, you are more than life to me. You are the air that I breathe, the first thing I think about when I wake and the last when I lay my head at night. My life no longer makes sense without you in it and all I want to do is love you until my last day on earth. You make me beyond happy, but would you make me, even more, happier by becoming my wife?" I said, holding a twenty-four-karat white platinum diamond encrusted engagement ring.

Honey looked at me in total disbelief. "Are you serious, Ky-mani?" she asked holding her hand over her mouth.

"Dead ass serious Honey. I love you," I said. Tears streamed down her face as she nodded yes.

I slipped the ring on her finger and kissed her deeply.

I gently made love to my soon to be wife and mother of my baby until morning broke. Life was perfect and nothing could change that!

Chapter Twelve
Monae

THIS BITCH WAS PREGNANT! Please, God, take me now because I just couldn't live with this bullshit. She was like a goddamn rat infestation that just wouldn't let up. How could they still be together after all the shit that's happened to them? It was like no matter what he wasn't letting her ass go.

The way his face lit up and shone when he announced her pregnancy. The smile he gave me sent chills down my spine. It was a good riddance kind of smile. He knew that I knew I was dead to him at that point. I no longer had anything to hold over him and her head. If anything, his smile let me know that he did that shit on purpose! He purposely got her pregnant, wanted her pregnant. That shit was like a gunshot to my soul.

It hurt more than hearing them fucking in the bathroom. This bitch won and I lost, I hated to lose. This was all becoming too damn much for me.

172

Both Angel and I sat there looking stupid as he and his family popped bottles and celebrated. It seemed to bother Angel a whole lot more since I knew she had been hounding Law about raising the baby as a family. She looked finished and she was my ticket to breaking them up. Now she had no shit on Honey.

"He never celebrated when he found out I was pregnant," Angel said as she stared at him dancing and smiling after giving his announcement. "He was mad as hell and broke up most of his shit. All he kept worrying about was Honey leaving him. But look at him, you would think that's his first child," she said before looking down at the floor.

"Really? He was happy when I was pregnant," I lied because I didn't want to feel how she did but she looked at me and laughed.

"Yeah, good one, Monae. He used to fuck someone I knew when you were pregnant and all I heard was that he wasn't pleased a thot was having his kids. His words not mine," she said and laughed.

I was too embarrassed to respond so I just got up and went to bed. I tried to sleep after my shower but they were making so much fucking noise. I laid in my bed and stared up at the ceiling. Angel wasn't lying. I remembered how Law literally hated my ass when he found out I was pregnant. He called me all kinds of bitches and accused me of trapping his ass and being sneaky. I wished I did trap him but he kept his ass free.

He used to send my ass to answerphone whenever I called him. He straight hated me. But I guess because I had finally gotten pregnant for someone I wanted to after all I had gone through; I didn't let it bother me because I was sure that eventually he would get with the program. But he never did.

The way he celebrated ached my heart. Why couldn't it have been me?! As I stared up at the ceiling, I wished I could go up the stairs and murder that bitch in her sleep. I fell asleep with a satisfying smile on my face as I imagined ending her life.

In the morning, I was relieved to see that Honey was still up in her room, I don't think I was ready to face the bitch that I wished I was. My life would be so complete if I could live her life.

174

Ky-mani spent most of the morning running around grabbing everything in his path that he thought would make Honey happy. He was making such a damn fuss about her, it was sickening.

Even the kids were running around excited. He had explained to them already that they were going to have a new brother or sister. It was all they spoke about for hours, I wanted to tell them to shut the fuck up but I knew Ky-mani would have whopped my ass.

Eventually Honey brought her uppity ass downstairs. Momma Doreen fussed around her as well as the rest of the family. Ky-mani doted on her like she was a prized Jewel or something. He pulled the chair out for her and stroked her face when she sat. I wanted to vomit. He even protected her stomach when Mani tried to climb on her. Angel sat beside me all in her thoughts.

"Do you see the way he caters to her? He never ever does me like that. All he ever does is ask me questions about the baby, what I ate, if there was anything he needed to know about the baby but that was as far as it went. But look," she said, pointing at them. "Look at the way he pays attention to her. It's more than just the baby; it's her too. He makes sure

175

she's ok, he feeds her and tends to her. Did you see the way he stroked her face and rubbed her back?" she said and I rolled my eyes.

I turned my back to them and she followed me. Fuck them.

"Angel, he may be happy about her being pregnant but her ass is no different from us. I heard that bitch begging for dick in the bathroom," I said and Angel stared at me.

"Shut the fuck up," she laughed.

"No lie. She was in there begging his ass for some dick and he fucked her ass in the bathroom. I caught them. So, fuck what you see now, my ass knows what's the truth and that bitch is just like us," I said and Angel laughed.

Ok, I knew I was lying out of my ass but Angel didn't need to know that. She may want to admit defeat and mope about their asses but I damn sure wasn't. I wasn't accepting shit.

I could see that she was relishing on what I said even if it was a lie. I saw Law camping outside waiting for Honey. I watched him from the stairs. He rushed in that bathroom before she even finished opening the door. I went up to the door after he closed it and I heard her telling him no but he begged her not to stop him. I heard him ask her to please allow it and she did.

When I heard him grunting and expressing how much he missed and loved her, my stomach turned. I didn't need shit in that bathroom but I thought he would have stopped knowing someone was outside but he didn't give a shit. He wanted her and wasn't anything stopping him from getting the pussy.

She looked uncomfortable to see me but he just didn't give a fuck, he even smiled at me as he passed with her.

I never thought things would have ended like this when I made that choice back then to have Chyna. All I wanted was Law and I couldn't see past that.

Angel and I sat and cracked jokes about Honey. I guess we must have forgotten where we were at because when we turned back around, I assumed that they heard us by the mean looks on their faces. Honey shook her head and stood to her feet to walk away but Ky-mani stopped her.

"You no good, pussy bitches," he yelled, walking towards us.

"Ky-mani!" his momma called him and he

177

stopped. She motioned for him to sit and he did.

"Honey," she said and I looked up at Honey.

She went to walk away and Angel and I laughed.
But then she turned to face us again and approached
us. I instantly put my hand up around my throat. That
bitch wasn't hitting my ass again.

"Y'all are some weak ass bitches," she snarled
at us.

"You better get them!" Momma Doreen yelled.
And I saw that all eyes were on us.

"So I beg for dick? What the fuck I need to beg
dick for? Let me school you two bitches. Good pussy
doesn't need to beg for dick," she yelled.

"Ow!" Momma Doreen yelled.

"I ain't begged a nigga to fuck me yet. And I
damn sure don't need to lie on my pussy and post fake
ass pictures, bitch!" she threw her words at me.

"Ain't no nigga fucked my ass and then denied
me. Beg dick? What like you two? Monae your ass
locked him in your house, talking about you will
open the door if he fucks you," she pointed at me.

"And you, Angel, talking about he ain't gone see
his baby if he doesn't fuck you. And I'm begging

dick? Bitches, please. You motherfuckers can't talk to me! Don't watch my pussy, bitches, it's on a level you motherfuckers could never comprehend. I can't help that my pussy fits his dick like a motherfucking key. Kids can't keep a nigga bitch; good pussy keeps a nigga! I left his ass alone and he still didn't want any of y'all. You wanna come for me? What you think because there's two of you that I'm scared? I ain't scared of nobody!!! Especially not your weak ass Monae who can't even take one punch," she scoffed at me.

"Y'all motherfuckers want to come for me, you better be on a level! You think y'all can do me? Well, I'm about to done both y'all," she pointed at us both.

"Done their asses baby," Momma Doreen cheered her on.

"Finish them!" Drake shouted in a fucking deep voice sounding like fucking Mortal Kombat.

"Monae, your ass got pregnant getting fucked in his office. And Angel, your ass got pregnant getting fucked at the back of his club. But my ass got pregnant by a dick I owned! Y'all motherfuckers forgot I was living in his house, sleeping in his bed as his woman, and driving his car! Y'all motherfuckers

179

can't step to me. I'm the motherfucking Queen Bee and they call me Honey! And my name is written all up and down that dick bitches," she shut our asses down.

She turned to walk away but turned to face us again.

"Oh and I can't beg for what I own bitches," she said, lifting her left hand and damn near blinding us with the rock on her finger. That fucker was so big; I was surprised she could lift her hand to show us.

I couldn't even move. Not only did he get her pregnant but he proposed to her too.

She walked away from us leaving us looking like damn fools.

"Damn, Law, you definitely dropped a seed off in her ass. Ma is a goddamn thug, a boss lady. Your seed making her mean just like yo' ass," Ricky laughed and Ky-mani dapped him up.

"Y'all motherfuckers had that coming. She ain't done nothing to you since being here but y'all been at her head, talking all kinds of shit about her. Now hear my warning. Leave my daughter-in-law or your asses will have me to deal with me. Feel me?" Momma

Doreen approached us and said. We both nodded our heads.

Angel didn't say a word; she just got up and walked away. I was too embarrassed to sit out there, so I walked away too.

I can't believe he told Honey that he used to fuck me in his office. This whole time I had been popping style on her, acting like me and Law was more than she thought and she knew I was just a fuck in his office the whole time. Law humiliated me by exposing that information to her.

I paced my bedroom floor trying to figure out what to do next. She had to pay for what she said. She had no right to lay my shit out for everyone to hear and especially not Angel. How could he ask Honey to marry him?

Angel was right when she said it was about Honey more than the baby. He loved her ass and I hated her because of it.

I tried to call Killa to let him know but his phone was turned off. I warned him about helping me to end their relationship and I also told him what I would do if he failed. I couldn't wait anymore; things were taking too long for my liking.

I was done waiting because things only seemed to get worse. When I first started fucking Killa, Honey was just Law's woman. Now she was his soon to be baby momma and wife!

The bitch wasn't even supposed to be here. Yeah, I started fucking Blacka too, sue me. I needed Law in my life and there wasn't anything I wouldn't do to achieve it, even if it meant fucking two cousins. I gave Blacka the code and told him Killa's plans. I was able to get the code the day I met Honey. I purposely set the alarms off by opening the doors and when Law kept deactivating it, I saw the code.

I gave it to Blacka because I wanted him to send someone else because I knew Law may look over a woman dipping back in her ex but a complete stranger would be Honey being a damn hoe. Plus, I was hoping maybe the nigga would kill her.

But by the looks of things, I guess it either didn't happen or Law just did not care. And now I knew the reason why we were all out there...Her ass!

I could no longer sit back and do nothing...Honey had to die.

I stayed in my room for the rest of the night and most of the next morning. I only emerged when I heard Law going ballistic downstairs. Something was up and I wanted to know what.

"Where the fuck is that bitch?!" he growled, smashing a chair against the wall. He looked like he had morphed into the fucking Hulk, the way he was heaving.

"Monae, have you seen Angel?" he barked at me and I shook my head. I had not seen her since we both had our asses handed to us by Honey.

So, where the fuck could this bitch be?

***

A few hours later and I saw Angel walking across the grounds. I didn't give a fuck where she had been at; I just wanted to see what Law was going to do about it. I quietly left my room and headed downstairs.

Angel tried to sneak back in but Law was camped out by the door waiting for her. As soon as she stepped one foot in, he was on that ass.

"Angel, where the fuck you been?" he shouted but then stopped. He just stood frozen, staring at her.

I wondered why until I looked down and saw what for myself. Her baby bump was gone. Angel wasn't a tall girl so you could have clearly seen her six- month pregnant belly but now that shit was almost as flat as mine!

Law lost his cool and grabbed her by the throat. His boys tried to loosen his grip but he wasn't letting go.

"Bitch, what the fuck happened to your belly? Did you kill my seed?!" he yelled into her face.

She couldn't even answer him the way he was cutting off her air. She faintly nodded her head and he dropped her. He pulled his gun from his waist and held to her head.

Angel sat coughing and choking, crying on the floor. "I'm sorry," she cried.

"Bitch, you killed my seed and all can say is sorry? Why, Angel?" he demanded.

"Because I knew that you would never love me and cater to me like you do Honey. I kept the baby hoping it would have brought us closer and together. But when I told you, you were mad breaking shit. But

184

Honey ends up pregnant and you were happy and celebrating. With Honey pregnant, I just knew you wouldn't want me anymore. I love you, Law, and I want all of you but it's clear who you want," she cried.

"So you killed my baby because you wanted me?! I knew your ass came out about it because of Honey. Your ass drove me crazy, pulling all kinds stunts. Upsetting Honey and all that bullshit, for you to just go and kill my child like that? How could you be so fucking, wicked, Angel? She was a baby, a full grown, kicking, hearing, and moving baby. How the fuck could you?!" he said, cocking the gun back.

"I'm sorry! I regretted it the second I did it but it was too late. Why couldn't you just want me like you do her? And now you're engaged to her. Didn't you think that would hurt me?"

"Bitch, I could care less. I told you from the jump what this was and what this would ever be between us. Your ass pursued me, talking about you know and you're cool with that and not looking nothing else but some dick. I never ever told you it was anything else, Angel, so fuck your damn feelings because you choose to catch them knowing full well you were nothing more than something to fucking do.

185

Even if I never met Honey, I still wouldn't want your ass."

"You killed my daughter for your own selfish reasons and I should end your fucking life right here, but instead I'm gonna let you live so that every fucking day you can live with the fuckries that you just did. But I tell you this," he said, bending down to meet her face.

"Don't you ever bring your ass around me again. After this day, you are dead to me and fuck with me, and I will make that true," he said, standing back up.

"Angel, since your ass is no longer pregnant with my seed and that was the only reason why you were here, your ass is out of here at first light, so pack up your shit," he said and walked away leaving her on the floor crying.

"Stupid ass bitch," I moaned looking at her. She was fucking useless to me now. Her leverage over Law was gone and any leverage was better than none. Now I was on my fucking own because of that weak bitch.

I went to my room and paced my floor. There was just no way I could be around her and watch Law loving his woman. They walked around here smiling and shit planning their wedding. She wanted to wait until the baby was born but he wanted it done now. Shit if he could have married her the same night he asked, he would. And I for one just could not let that happen. I could not just let it go.

The second I fell pregnant with Chyna, Law belonged to me. I should be the only mother to his kids and should be his fucking wife. After all the shit I did to have those fucking kids, I deserved to be his wife.

And since I wasn't, I damn sure wasn't going to allow him to have that with anyone, especially not Honey. That bitch dissed me with her very presence.

I wanted the satisfaction of seeing them break up but at that point, I would take any way that ended with them not being together. And since he just wouldn't let go and voluntarily leave her alone, I was going to make him involuntarily do it.

Me: Are you still interested in helping me get rid of Honey?

312-241-6754: For real, ma, I got you. When and where?

Me: Two weeks from today. Just enough time for me

to find somewhere to go with my kids.

Oh no, she wasn't? You must be saying but oh yes I was. I was ordering a hit on Honey. Tried to be nice about it and help her leave Law alone but she just wouldn't. So now she had to die. What? Didn't I tell y'all from the jump that this bitch had to die?

Y'all thought I was playing. I would have rather seen them apart and her suffering or knowing the fact that I was fucking him instead. But things never worked out like that, so she had to go.

I walked around that bitch smiling my ass off. Law kept his word and dragged Angel out of here kicking and screaming.

I sat and smiled at him and Honey showing affection, him rubbing hernone existent belly and jumping through hoops for her because I knew in less than two weeks, all that shit would be a memory. And then I would step in and comfort his ass and if he still didn't want me, then oh well, at least she wouldn't have him.

But then two days later, it all went terribly, terribly wrong!

Chapter Thirteen
Law

A nigga like me was in heaven. Despite Angel killing my fucking seed, I was happy with Honey. She was six weeks pregnant and going well. I could just imagine how beautiful our baby would be looking at Honey. She was the epitome of the word both inside and out. I couldn't love her anymore even if I tried.

It felt so damn good seeing her plan our wedding with my sisters. She wanted to wait until she gave birth but I just wanted her to have my last name immediately. If I could have married her ass in the morning I would.

Angel was just a trifling bitch. She had no right to do that shit and so far along in her pregnancy. I wish I knew the doc who did it so I couldn't end their fucking life for doing it. If anything, Honey had a right to do that because she didn't want to have a baby and she got pregnant because my trifling ass busted a nut

189

in her without her permission or knowledge but she hadn't. There was nothing Angel could have said to justify her actions about I would never love her like I did Honey, damn fucking right.

She played my ass though because I believed her when she said she was cool with whatever and was only interested in dick. She told me she wasn't like other females and so I believed her. But the bitch gets pregnant and forgets all that shit she was spitting before.

She acted like I promised her something. I should have beaten her ass when she told me she was pregnant. I knew I had did it to her a few times raw but I knew she told my ass she was on them shots otherwise my ass sure wouldn't have done it. But she told me it couldn't happen and even said if it did, she would dead that shit.

But yet the bitch ends up pregnant and keeps the baby.

I guess bitches would say anything to get the dick. But not my baby. I knew her ass loved me even when I fucked her off. And I knew she be loving my dick from all the hollering she would be doing but despite that Honey kept it hundred with me. She never

190

told me what I wanted to hear to please me or to get dick. Her ass pleased herself first even when I gave her the dick and a nigga could never be mad about that. Because with Honey, I knew her no was that and her yes was motherfucking yes, no other way around it. She was a sure thing.

Monae finally shut the fuck up. When Honey shut her and Angel down I was so fucking happy. That's exactly what that bitch needed because she instantly turned into a fucking church mouse. I ain't heard that bitch talk since and I couldn't be happier.

Life was sweet and everything was falling into place the only thing I needed to do was find out who this nigga The Don was and end his life. But for now, I would enjoy the peace and my fiancée being pregnant. Felt good as fuck to say that.

"Honey, how did the baby get in your stomach? Did you swallow it?" Mani asked making us all laugh. That's my boy thinking outside the box.

"No, Mani, I didn't swallow the baby. But that's where they grow like a flower grows in the soil," she laughed.

"Oh ok. You planted it?" he said, smiling.

191

"Something like that, yeah," Honey laughed.

"So if the baby is in your stomach, how can it be daddy's baby too? Did he plant it in there too?" Chyna said, looking at us.

"Um, who wants some ice cream?" I asked and everybody laughed. Now how the hell was I going to explain how I 'planted' my baby in Honey?

Yeah, they didn't need to know all that just yet.

We sat down as a family and enjoyed our dinner. Monae kept in her corner quiet and without any drama. I guess she was lost without her ratchet friend in crime – Angel.

Afterward, I tucked the kids into bed. Monae stood silently watching me the whole time, I knew she had something to say but she didn't.

When I made it to my room, Honey had just stepped out the shower and was standing there in a towel only. I approached her and pulled the towel away. I kissed and spoke to her belly for a minute, before devouring her sweet nectar and making our bodies become one.

192

I sat admiring Honey's naked body as she looked out of the window at the moonlight. I laughed at her little pudge that was trying to surface. My baby was pregnant!!! Yeah, I know you all were tired of me saying that but please allow me to stay on my cloud a little longer.

Right now, I had my momma, my sisters, my Unc, my brothers Drake, Ricky and KY, my beautiful kids and now my soon to be wife, all under the same roof. We were in a fucked up position with this Don shit but we were together and happy regardless.

And then…

"Um, Ky-mani, why is Monae outside? It looks like she's leaving." Honey said. I furrowed my brows and slowly sat up. Something inside me was telling me something wasn't right. I quickly rolled out of bed and into my closet. I pressed a button that flipped up a wall panel and showed me my monitors.

"Fuck!" I spat as I saw about ten niggas outside with guns about to walk in the house. I quickly hit the alarm to alert my family and grabbed some clothes. I ran and grabbed Honey and pulled her in the closet with me too.

193

"Bae, what's going on?" she said as I quickly helped her to pull clothes on. I grabbed my bullet proof vest and yanked it on her and that's when I heard the first sets of gunshots going off.

Honey screamed and started crying. I grabbed a couple guns, pushing one in my Jordans, one in my back, and one on either side and one in my hand.

I could hear gunshots ringing through the house and I knew my niggas were fighting back. All I could do was pray my momma and sisters got out. I pulled Honey towards the door and opened it slowly. The lights were out from the niggas cutting the electric. I pulled Honey down to the floor and kissed all over her face.

"Baby, listen to me. I need you to just get out and run and don't stop—" I started.
"No, no. I'm not leaving you," she cried, hanging on to me. She jumped when another shot rang off but this time closer to us.
"Baby, listen to me. I promise I will find you. But I gotta stay so you can have a chance to go. I will hold them off but you gotta promise me that you'll run," I said and she nodded crying her eyes out. I

kissed her all over her face and mouth and kissed her belly when I pulled her to her feet.

"Go down those stairs there and it should lead you out to the cars. Take mine and go," I handed her a small pistol just in case and gave her one final kiss.

She took off running back into our room and came out with two more vests and ran in the opposite direction.

"Fuck, Honey, listen to me and go!" I yelled.

"Not without the kids," she said. My heart dropped into the pit of my stomach. Monae left my kids?!

"Monae was alone, Ky-mani," she said. I grabbed her hand and took off towards my kids' room.

One nigga turned the corner as we reached and I sent one shot to his head.

"Get them and go right now!" I told her just as another one came and I sent two shots his way; one in the stomach and one to the head.

I let go of her hand and prayed that God would spare her and my kids. I looked back at her as she

195

went into their room and hoped that I will see her again.

I snuck down the hall with two guns drawn. I made it down the stairs to find three niggas standing. I dived to the floor and raised both guns, shooting and killing two. I scattered behind some furniture, just as the third one bust a shot just missing my head. I stuck my hand out and shot him in his leg and when he bent over, I shot him in the head.

Before I could turn around, I was shot in my shoulder making me drop to the ground and drop my gun.

"Fuck! Ahhh!" I yelled out as the metal burned my skin. I clambered behind the sofa as I heard his heavy footsteps approaching me. He stood in front of me and raised his gun at my head.

Sorry, Honey.

Pow! Pow! Pow!

Rang out and his body dropped to the floor. I pulled myself up and saw Honey pointing a gun.

"Baby, please come with us," she cried out. I

rushed over and pulled her into my arms. I looked down and my kids were under a table with vests on crying their eyes out.

I heard footsteps coming towards us but no other sounds of gunfire. Either my family got out or God forbid they were dead. Honey grabbed Mani and I grabbed Chyna and we took off running.

"Hold on to daddy's neck," I instructed Chyna and pulled a gun with my good hand. I turned my arm back and busted shots as I saw more niggas file into the house. Honey quickly unlocked the car and I handed her Chyna as she pushed Mani inside. I pulled another gun and shot at the house hoping it would buy us some time to get in.

Once I saw Honey climb in. I jumped in the car and locked the doors.

Bullets riddled the car as I started the car.

Honey jumped over into the back to shield the kids.

"It's bulletproof," I let her know and pushed my foot down letting the tires burn as I fled.

Honey sat hugging the kids and rocking them trying to stop them from screaming.

197

"Fuck!!!!" I roared and punched the steering wheel.

Who the fuck were those niggas? How could Monae set us up like that? She practically left my family to die. If Honey never saw her, those niggas would have come into the night and murdered us.

My head was spinning I couldn't think straight. I heard gunfire earlier so I know my boys and Unc were fighting back but then it all went quiet.

God, please no.

Eventually Honey got the kids quiet and they fell asleep. She climbed back on the passenger side and looked at me. She was still shaking and crying. I just hoped this wouldn't let her lose my seed. She grabbed some paper towels from the glove compartment and pressed it on my gunshot wound.

"Ky-mani," she said and when I looked at her, her eyes spoke volumes.

"They got out," I told her and she just stared at me.

After I checked that no one was following us, I pressed the dashboard. There were two lights lit; one showing the car we were in and one showing another of the cars was being driven.

The Range I was in was one of my four armored cars that I had made for an event like this. I made them linked so I could track each one and communicate between them. So, from the dash it was showing someone from my family was in one.

I pressed the communicator so I could speak to whoever was in the other car.

"Hello?" I heard my Unc's voice and I almost cried tears of joy.

"Yo, Unc, y'all ok?"

"Ky-mani!!!" I heard my momma, aunt, and sisters' voice calling me.

Thank God.

"Yo, nephew what the fuck happened, man? We barely got out. I got shot in my leg but I'm ok. So are the girls. They all got out fine."

"Where's the boys?" I asked and they went quiet.

"Ky-mani, they killed KY," Nevaeh said. I'm a thug ass nigga but that shit made me cry.

"No!" Honey said, crying. I grabbed her hand and kissed the back of it.

"They shot Drake too but we got him. But he won't wake up, Ky-mani," Nevaeh said.

"Fuck!" I punched the steering wheel and cried.

"And Ricky? Y'all please don't tell me he's gone too?" I sniffed and wiped my eyes with the back of my hand.

"We don't know, Ky-mani. We couldn't find him. He was with KY at one point when we were trying to get out. They shot Drake as we got out the door and that's when we saw them shoot KY in the head but we couldn't see Ricky," my Unc explained.

"Y'all go somewhere safe, please. Me, Honey, and the kids are going to hide somewhere. Y'all stay together, please. And Unc you already know no contact with anyone except me. Get a medical team for Drake. You still have that burner phone, Unc?"

"Yeah I do."

"Good. I will call you from it when I stop somewhere," I sniffed.

"Baby girl, you ok?" Unc said, asking Honey.

"Yeah, Marco, I'm ok. I'm not hurt or anything."

200

"Ky-mani, where's Monae?" Aunt Ruth asked.

"She's the one who sent them there. She took off as they started entering the house. She didn't even take the kids," I let them know.

"Oh my God, Ky-mani," my momma said.

"It's ok; we got them. Look I gotta go. Cameron was supposed to be meeting us in the morning. I gotta make sure he doesn't come down to Miami," I let them know.

"I'm glad y'all are all ok. Please be safe and I love you all. Drake come back to me, my nigga," I said, hoping he would hear me and do just that.

I ended the call with my family and shed some tears for my niggas and prayed for KY's soul.

I was abruptly pulled out of my sadness when I remembered Monae.

"Honey, I need to ask you something serious," I said, looking at her quickly before turning my attention back to the road.

"How would you feel if I asked you to be the kids' mother?" I said.

201

"They're already mine, Ky-mani. You know how much I love them," she said and I knew she wasn't lying. She ran straight for my kids and pulled vests on them to protect them. And when those niggas started shooting at my car, she covered them with her body without even second guessing. I knew without a doubt that she loved them as her own.

"Good because Monae can't live after this." And I was dead ass serious.

I made a call to one of my loyal little niggas and had him go over to Monae's house and see what he could find out. I also wanted him to sit on it for a few days to see if she returned. And if she did, I ordered him to kill her. I would have preferred to do it myself but for now, I no longer lived in Chicago.

I called one of my lieutenants and told him to shut everything down and get the fuck out. I wanted all my businesses and traps shut down immediately and all my niggas to go into hiding. Thank goodness I emptied my safes and deposited all my money in my bank before I had to flee to Miami, so I told my lieutenant to distribute whatever money was in the trap houses amongst my niggas so they could go underground. My last call was to Cam.

"Hello?" he said as the car number was blocked and untraceable. "Yo, Cam. It's me."

"Oh, what up, Cuz? I'm looking forward to coming tomorrow. I'm just at home packing my shit, nigga," he laughed.

"Cam, you need to go somewhere and lay low, my nigga. Some niggas just raided my house; killed KY, shot Drake, and may have killed Ricky too, he's missing."

"Yo, Law. What the fuck you talking about, dog?" I heard his voice crack.

"They came after us, my nigga. Monae's bitch ass lead them to us. We barely got out."

"Man, didn't I tell you about that hoe?" he said angrily and from his voice and constant sniffles I knew he was crying.

"Where my brother, yo?" he sniffed.

"I don't know, Cam," I said and he broke down.

"That's fucked up. And my Pops? My momma? Everybody else?" he asked.

"Unc got hit in the leg but he said he's straight and Aunt Ruth is good. All the girls are good. I got hit in the shoulder but I'm aight."

"Where you going, my nigga. Should I come there?" he asked. Honey tapped my hand and shook her head no. I looked at her for a minute before I spoke.

"I don't know, Cam. I'm just driving, my nigga. I may find a hotel or something," I said. I was actually headed to another safe house in Tennessee.

"Alright, Cuz, I'mma wait until I hear from you. I might just go back to Atlanta and lay low," he said.

We made arrangements to speak soon and hung up.

"Why didn't you want me to tell Cam where we were going?"

"It's not Cameron. It's just that I don't believe Monae did this alone. She could have someone inside still and until we know what's really going on it's best if you trust no one but us in this car. Cam could unknowingly lead that snake right to you," she said and that made sense.

"Do you trust me?" she asked me but she didn't need to. Ma came back for me and killed that nigga who was about to shoot me. Of course, I trusted her.

"With my life, baby," I said.

204

"Good. Now I have a holiday home that I bought for my momma. It's in Louisiana. Now Monae knows you but she doesn't know me. They would never find us there. It's in my grandfather's name and it's the safest place for us now," she said and I smiled.

My baby was thugging up!

"What's the address?" I asked, showing her I trusted her choice.

She keyed it in and we sat back holding hands as we thanked God that we made it.

RIP ,my nigga. I remembered KY.

Chapter Fourteen

Monae

I know I majorly fucked up! That wasn't supposed to happen. When I texted The Don the address to the Miami house, it was to take out Honey only.

Yeah... I was fucking him too. I only started doing it because he assured me he had the means to get Honey out of Law's life. He told me that Law had stolen his woman once and that he wanted to get him back by helping me. I was too blinded by my desire for Law that I couldn't see that he had another motive behind helping me.

I didn't realize that until it was too late. He never wanted to kill Honey like he said he did. He just wanted to know where Law was and I led him right to him.

When he texted me asking what room the safes were in and if I knew the code, I knew something was up. First of all, his questions came across as if he could see the house. What wing and what floor? How would he know that?

So being paranoid, I left the kids sleeping in their beds and went to have a look. That's when I saw the house was literally sounded by men in black with guns. I had no choice but to run for my life. I didn't even have time to go back in to get the kids. I jumped in Ricky's car and took off.

My heart bled when I saw the lights go out and heard the first gunshots ring out.

All I could do was pray God spared my kids or let them die quickly. I know it sounds bad but Law didn't want my ass anyway, so having the kids didn't change that. No one was going to look out for me but me, so I had to do what was best for me.

And now I've been driving endlessly for hours. I have nowhere to go but one place – back to Pete.

After I left him, he moved to New York. He tried reaching out again once, which was how I knew where he lived. Maybe I did the right thing leaving the kids behind. He never knew about them and I knew he wouldn't accept me if I arrived with them.

As I headed out of state, I thought of all kinds of excuses to give him and prayed he accepted it. I left without my purse or anything. Nothing but my cell. So, if he didn't want me back – I was fucked!

Almost twenty hours later and I arrived at the address I had for him when he wrote me a letter, which I had stored on my cell – thank God.

I stopped at a gas station ten minutes away to freshen up a little. I didn't know if he had a woman and I didn't care.

I nervously approached the townhouse and knocked on the huge black door.

The few seconds that I stood waiting, felt like an eternity. Then I heard the doors being unlocked and then it opened. Pete stood there looking at me.

He looked older with gray hair in his beard but he looked the same. I had not seen him in eight years before I made it my mission to get Law.

"Monae, baby, I knew you would come back," he said, embracing me and pushing his tongue into my mouth.

On second thought – maybe they should have just killed me!

Honey

It took us almost twenty hours to arrive at the house in Louisiana. I bought it for my momma so she could vacation with my grandma, whenever they needed a break. It was in a quiet woodland overlooking a lake. There was a security shack at the beginning of the path, which was another reason why I bought it, so they would feel safe going out there.

I checked in with them and got the spare key since I didn't have my purse with me. Ky-mani was a little more prepared and had emergency cash and cell phones stashed in the car. We wasted no time getting the kids into the house. It was fully furnished and stocked with linens and towels. All we needed was food but I would sort that soon. We had stopped a few times along the way for restrooms and refreshments, so we had a little something to eat.

I ran a bath, set the kids in front of the TV, and assisted Ky-mani to undress to get in the bath. I cringed at the sight of the gunshot wound to his left shoulder.

"I'm ok, baby. How are you? No pains or issues?" he asked me.

"No nothing. I'm fine," I was a little shaken up

but I was fine.

He closed his eyes and sunk in the water. He asked for some alcohol, tweezers, and some bandages. I quickly grabbed them from a cupboard, checked on the kids and went back into the bathroom.

"Thank you, baby," Ky-mani said, sitting up straight.

He grabbed the alcohol and poured a good amount on the wound.

"Argh," he said through gritted teeth. He then pushed the tweezers into it after sanitizing it with a lighter.

"Ssss. He hissed as he rooted around until he found the bullet. He yanked it out and threw it in the trash can. He grabbed some patches and held it against it to stop the blood.

When it wasn't so bad, he poured more alcohol on it and I put a big waterproof bandage on it so he could finish bathing.

"How's my baby?" he asked me, stroking my face. I was so close to losing him. I shut my eyes and pictured that man standing over him with a gun pointed at him.

I told the kids to close their eyes and cover their ears before aiming my gun and shooting him. I had never shot anyone in my life before but I couldn't let him kill Ky-mani.

I didn't realize I was crying until I felt his hand wiping my tears off my face.

"That's the second time you've saved me. We are connected for life, Honey," he said, kissing me. Ky-mani was my world and I refused to live without him if I could help it. As for Monae – I would gladly kill her myself.

Ky-mani finished off in the bath and I bandaged his shoulder once he was dressed. I climbed in the sofa with the kids and wrapped them in my arms. I placed two kisses on their heads and hugged them close. I couldn't even imagine if something happened to them.

Ky-mani picked up the remote and started browsing the channels until something devastating caught our attention. There live on TV was a reporter outside of Ky-mani's club and it was on fire! She continued to explain the story and that's when we found out all his businesses were burned to the ground. I looked at him and his facial expression was one of pain and anger. He called the young man that he called last night and asked to find Monae.

So not to upset the kids, he took the call outside. I watched as he yelled into the phone and waved his arms around. When he finally ended the call, he slumped down on the patio step and dropped his head in his hands.

"Stay here, babies. I'm going to see about daddy. Ok?" I said and kissed them.

"Yes, momma Honey," they said and I turned to look at them. What they said made me smile instantly.

I opened the door, stepped out, and closed it quietly behind me. I joined him on the step and linked my arm in his. He kissed me softly on my head and sighed out.

"They burned down everything. They killed everybody, no one but Trigger is left. I told him to get out the country and hide. He didn't find Monae but he did find some other shit," he said.

"I always questioned how she got pregnant because I know I never slept with her unprotected. Trigger told me this hoe has my seeds frozen in her fucking freezer," he said, shaking his head.

Oh my God, I knew she was crazy but to have

his semen frozen like that.

She really impregnated herself with his sperm?

Wow.

"That's the least of my worries. How am I supposed to get at this nigga Don's head without my boys or crew? Me alone can't take him on but I have no choice. My Unc can't fight with me," he said.

"You're not alone baby. I think it's time I called on a few of my friends," I smiled and kissed him. "Can I borrow your phone please?" I smiled and he handed it to me.

I sent a quick text to Tasha.

Unknown: Code 10 – man down. H

"What's that mean?" Ky-mani, chuckled looking at what I sent.
"It's code that we made up to let each other know when one of us was hurt or in trouble. They will be here in a few days," I smiled and kissed his cheek.

I pulled him up to his feet and went inside to get

213

some food and prepare for our guests.

<u>Chapter Fifteen</u>
Law

Honey had something up her sleeves. She
bought a mad amount of food and blow up beds
like she was expecting an army. She said her peoples
were coming but I thought it was just her girls?

Two days later and the cabin phone rang letting
us know we had a visitor. Excitedly, Honey headed
down the path. She told me to wait, so I did. A few
minutes later and five cars pulled up outside.

The first car had Chase and the crazy
musketeers: Kelis, Sydney, and Tasha. They
hugged and dapped me as they went into the cabin.

The other cars were filled with mad niggas but I
only recognized Troy. "Yes, Cuz in law. We heard you
needed us, so we are here," he dapped me.
Honey approached me with a huge smile on her

face and kissed my lips and pulled me in. The whole room went quiet as I closed the door behind me.

"First thing: introductions," Honey said.

Troy stood first with about thirteen other niggas. "You know me, Law, but these are my brothers," he pointed to three men who looked similar to him. "And these are my boys that I roll with. We are not street but we can throw hands and fuck people up and we nice with guns too. We straight but we know people trust us. You showed me that you're willing to lay your life down for our cuz and would defend her at all costs. Well, we here to say the same to you. We not about to leave our cousin husband less and ain't no one out there for her but you," Troy said, holding his fist to his heart as well as all who stood with him.

I returned the gesture.

Next Chase stood to address me.

"I told you thugs stick together. I used to be something in my town in the Bronx, New York. These are my niggas," he said, pointing to the remaining ten niggas.

"They're crazy, sick motherfuckers but I think

you need a little crazy right about now. Honey is my sister. This fucker, The Don, fucked with her husband, so he fucked with me," he said and I nodded my head at him.

"May I, bae?" Honey asked permission to speak up. I smiled, nodded my head and folded my arms and watched as my baby bossed the fuck up.

"Ok now. TJ?" She called.

"Yep," a nigga who looked like Troy, but darker, spoke up.

"You're the governor of your prison. See if you can find out from your friends at the jail in Chicago if anyone knows who this nigga is," she ordered and her cousin started writing shit down in his notebook.

"Trevor?" she called out again and another brother answered.

"You own a security company, so any kind of surveillance would be good."

"On it, Cuzzo," he replied.

"Tremaine and Troy y'all in real estate. Act like you interested in buying property so that y'all can find out what's the word on the streets who to hit up. See if we can get an address for where The Don conducts his business. He wants to fuck with our food, we will fuck with his," I smiled because my baby was making me proud.

"Chase and crew, y'all will be the biggest key to this because y'all are new faces and from the streets. We need you to infiltrate his crew, join and earn their trust find out who is who and if they have any other plans for us," she said and they all agreed.

"And Gangsta Bitches?" she yelled out and them crazy females started dancing making everybody laugh. "Y'all need to be my eyes and ears. I already know you bitches are nosey so it should be easy for you," she said and they laughed.
"I wanna have info on that bitch, Monae. I wanna know who the fuck she was working with because clearly, the bitch isn't smart enough to do this alone. You may need to partner up with Chase's crew. Niggas might tell you if they know Monae and I bet my ass they do," she addressed both teams.

"I've created an email just for us, no one but us in this room will know it. We will keep in contact like that," she said, handing out a strip of paper to each crew.

"Laws enforcers at yahoo.com?" someone spoke out and we started laughing.

"Of course. They call my baby Law," she winked at me.

Once she was done, I gave them all addresses and places to scope out. I also gave them a list of people to check if they were still alive. I gave my pilot details to Chase's crew so they could travel back and forth to NY without any problems.

Once we finalized details, the girls cooked up a feast.

I never knew Honey knew people like this but I was glad to see they had her back no matter what.

Honey

I was overwhelmed when everybody turned up. It meant more to him than they would ever know. Tasha was the glue in this all because she wasted no time calling on Troy and letting him know that I needed help.

To see the masses of people who had our backs; Ky-mani's back, was priceless. But that nigga and Monae fucked with the wrong ones!

Troy and his people spent two days with us, working out the fine details before they left to get on it. Chase's crew went back to NY to ready some more niggas just in case The Don had a big crew.

Only my girls, the kids, Ky-mani, Chase, and me were left. It was a two- bedroom cabin; so, Ky-mani and I were in one with the kids on a blow up bed. Chase and Tasha in the other and Kelis shared the living room with Sydney.

Kelis was having a hard time knowing Drake was in a coma but every day it got better for her. Marco told us that he had some brain activity, so every day brought more hope. We held a little memorial for

KY in the back by the lake. Ky-mani was torn up about not being able to get his body.

We all said a piece for him, including Tasha, and y'all already know that they had a love-hate relationship. My fondest memory of him was when he was dancing at the barbecue.

Everybody laughed when I attempted to copy his dance moves.

Because I owned the property I was able to plant a tree in his memory. "To KY." We all toasted.

"Jelly," Tasha added and we all laughed.

"That nigga would find a way to come back from the dead to shoot your ass," I said laughing.

"My husband would protect me," she smiled. "Hell Nah," Chase said and we fell out laughing.

"He don't wanna be bothered with your ass. KY would be doing him a favor," Sydney said.

"What? I am a delight," Tasha said and we all sucked our teeth.

Some time later, Ky-mani was on the couch

watching TV with the kids and Chase was upstairs. My girls and I sat around the dining table gossiping.

"Bitch, that crazy bitch really sent gunmen into the house like that and left the kids?" Tasha said, shaking her head.

I know Ky-mani said they were there for him but I just couldn't shake the fact that maybe Monae meant for them to get me alone. She's done nothing but try her hardest to be with Ky-mani, she loves him in her own psychotic way but I just can't see her sending men in to kill him!

"So, bitch, I guess you lose the game of *pussy roulette*, with your pregnant ass," she whispered the game name so the kids wouldn't hear.

I just shook my head at her and kissed my teeth.

"Shame bitch," Sydney said and we all started laughing.

"How far are you, Honey?" Kelis asked.

"About six weeks."

"Oh. I guess we due around the same time," she said lowly.

The other girls looked at each other before

realizing what Kelis just said.

"Oh my God, Kelis. Did Drake know?" I asked and she shook her head.

"I found out before I came here," she sniffed.

"Bae!" I called Ky-mani and waved him over. He put Mani down and came over to us.

"Kelis is pregnant," I told him. He looked at Kelis shocked before smiling and giving her a big hug.

"I'mma tell Unc to let Drake know. I guarantee that will wake his ass up." Ky-mani smiled and kissed her cheek. He took his phone out and went into the back to call Marco.

I hugged Kelis and we rubbed each other's belly at the same time.

We continued to make small talk until Tasha hushed us. She held her hand out for us not to speak and listened. All of a sudden, she took off running upstairs. A few seconds later, we heard the sound of someone falling and we already knew it was Tasha's crazy ass.

We laughed when we heard Chase yell at her and ask her what was wrong with her.

223

"Everything," Sydney said and we coughed laughing. Seconds later, and Tasha was in the doorway coming towards us.

"I'm sure I don't wanna know, but what the fuck happened?" I said.

"I thought I heard the shower turn on. I ran upstairs to see Chase naked so I could see his dick," she said, looking at us like the shit she just said was normal.

Crazy ass hoe. I shook my head.

"But I fell over and almost broke my pussy," Tasha said and we all spat out laughing.

"What the hell is wrong with you? Why were you running like that anyway?" I shook my head and asked.

"Because we are here, he talking about I ain't getting none until we go home. He won't even let me see the dick," Tasha sucked her teeth and folded her arms.

"Hey, babe," Ky-mani called me and I looked up at him.

"I finally understand what you meant when you said your girls were wild. I don't think I've ever met a

224

chick crazier than Tasha. I ain't even lying," he shook his head and we all laughed.

If only he really knew!

****

Two days later and Chase's crew and my cousins were back. We wasted no time getting down to business. I fed and bathed the kids and settled next to Ky-mani to see what was up.

"Ok. Law, do you know this nigga?" Trevor said, handing us a photo. Ky-mani looked at it and shook his head no.

In the photo was a tall, dark skin man with an Afro, gold grills, gold chains, and rings.

"No, I don't know that nigga, why?"

"That's The Don, and boy does he have a hard-on for you," Trevor said.

"Yeah. Apparently, he wants everything you own," Chase said.

"We found out that he's operating out of Killa's club. Killa is nowhere to be found and his cousin, Blacka, who funded it was found dead." Troy said.

"Killa is in jail," TJ said and I shook my head. "I had a few wardens in the county jail ask around about The Don and sure enough, Killa surfaced. Apparently, he tried to kill one of the hoes he was seeing who ended up pregnant for him. I'm sorry to tell you this, Honey, but according to Killa, she was the one who burnt your house down," he said to me and my stomach felt sick.

Jerome spent all his time cheating on me and to know that it was someone he cheating on me with, who tried to kill me, left me feeling weak!

Ky-mani rubbed my hand and kissed my lips. I smiled and dropped my head on his shoulder.

"Ok, so The Don has about 20 men around him. They aren't the smartest niggas ever and his operation isn't shit. But I believe he's got one of your men on the inside because word on the streets is that your men were wiped out by someone they knew. No one from your list was alive, Law," Turbo said. He was one of Chase's men from the Bronx.

"That would explain why they all died like that. They would have been unarmed if they knew the person, making them easy targets. I can't even think of who it could be helping The Don," Ky-mani said.

"Ky-mani, there are two other things that you need to know," Troy said before looking over at Chase, who nodded his head.

"First of all, we found Monae. She's in New York with some old nigga called Pete. We had her photo circulating through our channel of niggas and they came back with this," Chase handed over a photo. It was of Monae, sporting a conspicuous, blonde wig. I couldn't help the smile that crept across my face and when I looked up, Ky-mani had the same one!

"Now that is good news," Ky-mani smiled.
"Yeah but we found out she was fucking Killa because she wanted him to get rid of Honey, and she was fucking Blacka and The Don too. She was the one who gave out the code to your crib," I felt something stir in me as I heard Turbo say that. And like I had said those men were sent to Miami for me!

Ky-mani pulled me into his lap and kissed my lips. "As long as I'm breathing, nobody is going to

227

hurt you," he said and I nodded.

"And also, Ricky is alive," Chase said and Ky-mani popped his head up.

"My dude, please tell me you're not joking," he asked eagerly.

"No, he's alive but they keeping him locked up somewhere. Apparently, The Don wants him so he can get your formula, Law. This is what this whole thing is about. He wants your empire," Chase explained.

Ky-mani nodded his head and put his head down in my chest. The whole room went quiet as everybody went into their thoughts.

"Ok, ok, we gotta make a plan," I said and everyone nodded to agree.

"We need to flush out this nigga and I think I know how," I said and everyone looked at me.

"Baby, you're what he wants. Maybe it's time to show your face in Chicago. Chase, if you have more men you should bring them now, make them blend in as regular everyday people but they will be there with Ky-mani so that if and when anything pops off, they will be there. But he's gotta look like he's alone," I said hopeful.

"That's actually not a bad idea, ma," Ky-mani said and kissed my cheek.

"Oh, shit we about to do this," Chase said and everyone started to laugh.

"Oh, we ready," Turbo said, picking up a big black duffle bag and dumping its contents on the table. It was filled with all kinds of guns, knives, and weapons.

Chase's face lit up as well as every nigga in the room.

"And I got three more bags of this shit, in the car." Turbo let known. Everybody started picking up their weapon of choice.

Ky-mani went for the assault rifles, Chase the blades, Turbo the shotguns, and Troy with the handguns. But what we didn't expect was Tasha's crazy ass to pick up something off the table.

"Man, I swear, if I never went to church I would have been an assassin. I swear; I even dream that shit!" she said.

Everybody looked around at each other before we busted out laughing.

"Bitch, I'm done with your loony ass. You're a got damn wanna be hoe, stripper, and now a fucking assassin. Chase, what the fuck you been feeding this crazy hoe?" I said with tears as I was laughing that hard.

"Nigga, I don't go church but I'm gonna make an exception for you and start praying for your ass," Ky-mani said and we all continued to laugh.

I know we were about to head off into the unknown and some of us could potentially end up losing our lives, but it was a good feeling being amongst them and laughing.

"Y'all from the bottom of my heart, I truly appreciate each and every one of you, especially you, baby. You've been my strength and I wouldn't be here without you. I know we about to head off with this motherfucker and shit is about to get real but I just want to do something first, if that's alright with y'all?" Ky-mani asked.

"Sure thing, Law." Troy and Chase said and everyone else nodded to agree.

"Honey, would you like to marry me in the next few days?" Ky-mani asked me.

I jumped to my feet and hugged on to him.

230

"Of course!" I squealed and everybody cheered.

Like I said these were some fucked up times but let's take some time out and get married y'all!

Chapter Sixteen
Law

It took us four days to set up the wedding and get all that Honey wanted and needed. Ideally, we would have wanted our family there too but I definitely didn't want to explain to her momma why we were in hiding, plus Drake was still out and couldn't be moved or left alone. But Honey and I decided that once it was all over and life spared, we would do a big wedding with the whole family.

I got me a little Armani black tux and Chase was my best man in a matching suit. The girls were bridesmaids in simple, but pretty, baby blue dresses. Mani carried the rings and Chyna was the little flower girl. We decorated the backyard with chairs, tables, an arch that I was standing under, and a white carpet for

Honey to walk down on.

Honey emerged from the house looking so fucking beautiful in a floor- length white satin dress that hugged her beautiful body. Her hair was in an elegant side braid with a white rose in it.

She smiled her big intoxicatingly sexy smile with her eyes sparkling like hazel diamonds as Troy walked her down the aisle to me.

When she made it beside me, I stroked her beautiful face. The hired Pastor started the ceremony and I kept my eyes on Honey.

When it was my time to speak, I spoke from my heart – thug or not.

"Honey, you came into my life when I needed you the most. I was lost but you found me and blessed my existence with your beautiful soul. I never knew love until I met you. You saved me in more than one way. I'm blessed to have you; the kids are blessed to have you and I'm blessed that you have honored me by giving me another child. I told you the other day that you and I are connected for life but even in death

233

my spirit will forever love you," I said and wiped the tears that fell from her eyes.

"Ky-mani, you say that I saved you but you saved me too; emotionally, physically and spiritually. You showed me a love that I never knew was even possible. You came to me at my lowest point and elevated me to my highest just by loving me. You came into my life and added to it with your wonderful being and our beautiful children. Thank you for loving me and picking me to carry another one of your precious gifts.

I could tell you how much I love you but even then, it wouldn't be enough; there're not enough words in the world that could describe how much you and the children mean to me. I promise to always be by your side. I love you, Ky-mani, more than life itself," she said and smiled.

The Pastor went on to bless our union until finally, I was able to kiss my wife! I pulled her in close, wrapped my arm snugly around her and made love to her mouth with mine.

Finally, Honey was my wife.

234

Everybody cheered loudly and threw rice on us.

We sat at the table eating, wrapped up in each other's arms. We partied until the early hours of the night until everybody left to a local hotel with the kids too.

"Ummm," Honey groaned as I sucked on her neck and pulled her dress off. I unhooked her bra and pulled a nipple into my mouth. I pulled my suit off and then my boxers. I ran my hand down Honey's body until I reached her white lace panties. I used my teeth and pulled them down, causing her to laugh and squirm.

She grabbed me and pushed me down on the bed. She took my hard dick and wrapped her juicy lips around it. She had never given me heads before but I loved how she reserved that just for her husband, so I wasn't mad.

She bobbed her head up and down on my shaft and I hissed with pleasure as it felt so fucking good. She wet it up real nice and sucked the shit out of the tip before deep throating my shit.

"Babyyyy, oh my God," I groaned as she did a

235

move that had my toes curling like a motherfucker.

"I'mma nut, Baby," I groaned and she stopped. It was my turn to return the favor.

I pulled her up to me and sat her on my face. "Argh!" she screamed and I laughed.

I sucked on my pussy as she rode my face.

"Ooohhhh," she cooed and shook. I put one hand on her ass and one on her breast. "Ky-mani, oh my God, baby," she said with her voice trembling.

She began to pant rapidly until she came all in my mouth. I licked up every drop before lifting her and sitting her on my dick.

We smashed our lips together as she rotated her hips deeply on my dick. "I love you, Mrs. Parker," I whispered, against her lips.

"I love you more, Mr. Parker," she groaned.

I spent two days making love to my wife and cementing our love for each other – until it was time to face my enemy!

***

Turbo, Chase, and their boys were the first ones to hit up Chicago. Peanut and about 10 of his goons came down from the Bronx to meet me. Peanut was a stocky nigga with brown braids, brown eyes, and a chocolate complexion. They would be my silent crew watching from the sideline. Troy and his brothers took my kids to my uncle and my momma. Honey stayed at the cabin with the girls until Troy went back there with them.

I wasn't nervous at all, as I finally touched down in Chicago. All I wanted to do was find The Don, kill him and find Ricky. I hit up Cameron on my way in and we arranged to meet up once he landed from ATL. But for now, I needed to make my presence known. I drove around the streets and made sure every nigga and bitch saw my face so they could go running back to The Don.

It burned me to see all my businesses to be nothing more than a pile of ash but vengeance would be mine.

I kept in contact with everyone using my burner phone. So, we wouldn't be caught on, Chase and the

Bronx crew were under my momma's name and Troy
with his people were my Aunt Ruth. I drove all around
my old spots trying to see if I could see but one
member of my old crew to see who the snake was;
because everyone else was dead, so only the snake
would be alive but I didn't see anyone I recognized.

I got a text from my 'momma' to say my
grandfather was looking for me, which meant The Don
had got wind I was in town and was on the hunt.

I shot a text back to say I was coming home
soon. That meant I was about to lay some niggas out. I
parked up my car near a house I was told a few of The
Don's niggas stayed at. As I was about to climb out my
car,
I noticed Peanut and his men scattered around
me. Some on the phone, some looking in store
windows like they about to shop, and some walking
with bad ass females they brought from the Bronx
looking like they were on dates.
I smirked to myself because my baby thought
of it all.

I looked behind me and noticed a park that was
covered by bushes and trees. I realized that would be

the perfect ambush spot. I looked up and noticed a few of The Don's niggas clocking my presence. Turbo was with them and a few of his men. They started pointing at me and suggested that they followed me. I bowed my head and turned to walk into the park.

And sure enough, the men started following me. I found the most covered section I could and waited there.

"Ayo, hold the fuck up. Well if it isn't the fallen King of Chicago," one short ugly Flava Flav looking nigga said to me, laughing.

I looked around and Turbo and his men gave a slight head nod. Next thing I knew, Chase ran up on the Flava Flav nigga and busted his throat open with a knife.

Turbo took out the nigga next to him with one shot as his boys and Peanut handled the others. We quickly dragged the bodies into the bush and Turbo called his clean-up crew.

"I didn't even have to move or use my gun," I chuckled. Them niggas were that quick. Just like my boys were.

"I told you this crew was whack as fuck and that The Don's operation was weak. The only advantage he had was the snake but that's it," Turbo said.

"Yeah I heard you but damn I was still expecting to bust some kind of moves," we all chuckled.

"You're the man and all but we ain't trying to get on Honey's bad side. She already warned our asses about you. You ain't allowed to do shit but go home safely," Chase said and we laughed.

"We gotta move fast now and they know you here. We about to go handle the rest of them in the house and the club; y'all get at The Don," Peanut said before skipping out with his niggas and a few from Turbo's team.

Now that we thinned out the crew, it was time to cut the head off the snake.

"One of my boys said The Don is at a strip club in the next town now with four men," Turbo said, looking at his burner phone.

"Alright, I need to get this nigga. And I need to find Ricky," I rubbed my chin and thought. I pulled out my phone and called Cameron. Luckily, he had landed and was heading my way.

I looked around at these men that I came to know and respect. Chase, Turbo, the seven remaining niggas and I headed back to our cars to gear up. I already had on my bullet proof vest, so I grabbed up another set of guns.

Before long and Cameron was pulling up his car alongside me. We embraced when he got out the car.

"My nigga, shit is crazy yo," he said looking around. I handed him a vest and gun too, and once everyone let it know that they were ready; we headed for the strip club!

Me, Chase, and Cam rode in silence. I guess we were all hopeful things would go smoothly and that we would get to go home to our women and family. I could see on Cam's face that he was worried about Ricky.

We stopped out back by the strip club and Turbo got out of his car. He took off to the front and then came back, a few seconds later. The rest of us got out the cars.

"Ok, he's in there. Are we ready?" he asked and I looked at Cam, who nodded yes at me. We drew our guns and headed inside.

As soon as we stepped inside, gunshots started ringing out. Turbo and Chase started bussing shots from behind a pillar. As the boys covered me, I dipped and dived deeper into the room to get closer to The Don. I laid out the nigga next to him, before sending a shot to The Don's left leg.

The rest of the boys and Cameron came over once they finished whoever else was with The Don. He looked up at me and flashed a cocky ass smile before I stomped him out cold. Turbo and Chase yoked his ass up and took him out through the back door.

Me, Cam, and the rest followed them out. They put a pillow case over his head and put him in the back of Turbo's van.

"Yo, Law, we got a warehouse out here," he said with a grin on his face.

"That's like music to my ears."

Since everything I owned was gone, including the warehouse, I had nowhere to take that nigga. Only my momma's house and the new house I had built for me and Honey, was still standing.

I got in my car and followed behind Turbo. He

242

led us to the pier where there was a string of warehouses by the dock. A gate opened and we drove in. Turbo jumped out and they pulled The Don out and dragged him into the warehouse.

"Oh shit, y'all done brought me to the candy store," I cheesed hard as I looked around at all the weaponry and tools that decorated the walls. There was a huge furnace at the back. They strapped the nigga to a chair and stood back. Everybody lit up a blunt and fixed their eyes on me with smiles on their faces.

"Shit, I've heard stories about you, nigga. I'm excited as fuck to see you in action," Chase said and everybody fell out laughing.

"No, you fucking don't. This nigga has been touched in the fucking head, he carved somebody's heart out their chest and he held it in his hand," Cam said, looking like he wanted to vomit.

"Thug life nigga," Chase laughed.

I walked around looking at the wall until I found my weapon of choice – a motherfucking pick axe!

I walked over to The Don and delivered a hard two hit combo to his jaw to wake his ass up.

243

"Argh motherfucker!" he spat blood from his mouth.

"Shut your punk ass up! You gunning for me, nigga?! You don't know who I am?!" I yelled.

"THEY CALL HIM LAW, MOTHERFUCKER!!!" everybody yelled out and laughed.

"Nigga, you came at my head with my momma in the house," I said, slicing him across his cheek with the axe. "My sisters," I sliced him on the other side. "My aunt and my Unc," I pulled my .9 and sent a shot in his left shoulder.

"My boys," I sent another shot in the right shoulder. "And my kids and pregnant wife!" I spat through clenched teeth and dropped the pick axe onto his left thigh.

"ARRRGGGHHHHHH!!!" he hollered. And when I lifted the axe, some of his flesh was hanging from it.

"Nigga, who in my camp are you working with and where is my cousin?" I grabbed him by his Afro and pulled his head up.

"Nigga, fuck you! You think I'm it? You have no

244

idea what's going on," he chuckled weakly. "You might as well kill me," he coughed.

"Nigga, where is my cousin!!!" I roared and choked him.

"In the last place, you would ever think to look," he laughed.

I raised the axe and hit him all over his body. He screamed out as the axe hit his body. I gave him one final hit before dropping it to the ground. I grabbed his hair again and lifted his head so he could look me in my eyes.

"This is for KY and Drake," I said before plunging my knife into his stomach and slicing him all the way up from his belly button to his throat.

"Damn!!!" everyone cried out.

"My nigga you need to get some professional help," Cam said and we laughed.

I cut The Don loose from the chair and dragged his disfigured body along the floor towards the furnace. I pressed the button to open it and Turbo and Chase helped me to lift him and drop him in.

"So what now, Law?" Chase asked as I washed my hands off.

"Now, I just want y'all to help me do one last sweep of the town, make sure no one else from that nigga's crew is still around and also, I want to make sure the two houses are safe before I bring my family back. Cam and I will look for Ricky and the snake. I got a feeling they hiding somewhere and passing information that way. I just need a few days and after that y'all can go back home," I said and they all agreed.

"But Chase can I ask one favor please?"

"Sure thing, Law."

"I think it's time I saw my baby momma," I said smiling. Monae was walking and breathing long enough!

***

A week later and all was back to normal as it could be. We never found any more niggas from The Don's crew and the houses were secure. I installed new security measures to both and Turbo and his men decided to move out here and be our security detail since he fell in love with the town. I burned down the club and all the properties that The Don had.

Turbo went down and got my momma, my sisters, my aunt and my Unc, as well as Drake who had finally woken up from his coma. He lost the feeling in his legs but the doctors were hopeful that it was just bruising and swelling from the bullet and felt in time he would regain movement.

He was happy to know Kelis was pregnant. I moved them into the guest house at my momma's.

Monae tried to hide but, eventually, Peanut found her. This bitch was sick as fuck. They found her living in a house with the old nigga she was seen with, dead in his bed. She cut his throat.

She was held up in the warehouse by the pier, that I bought off Turbo, but her I could deal with another time because I still hadn't found Ricky!

Cam and I drove around town looking everywhere but there was no sign of him.

I felt defeated and like I had let my cousin down
– until…

"Yo fuck me!" I yelled out and jumped to my
feet.

"What?!" Cam asked me.

I looked at him with wide eyes and my mouth
just as wide open. It never hit me until that point.

"I think I know where Ricky is," I said,
smacking my forehead. "That nigga said he's in the
last place I would ever think to look. Back in the day
when I first started out, we used to run shit from a
barn out back from Papa De's crib. He lives on an
island now but the property is still there!" I said,
rushing up the stairs to Honey who was putting the kids
to bed.

"I have to go. I think I know where Ricky is. I
want you to know that I love you more than anything
in this world. Nothing but you, my kids, and our new
baby, means everything to me. I promise this will be it
and then we can finally focus on us and plan that
wedding that you deserve," I said, kissing her all over
her face.

"Don't talk like that, Ky-mani. You're coming back to us or I swear I will find a way to kill you myself and haunt your got damn ghost for the rest of my life. I'm a part of some crazy ass bitches so you know we will find a way," she said and I laughed.

"Hell no please, not Tasha's ass," I laughed and she smacked me.

"I love you, Ky-mani, and be safe please," she pouted before kissing me deeply and passionately.

Man, if I wasn't trying to rush to find Ricky, I would have crept up in her guts!

We broke our kiss and I dashed out the room. I went into my safe and grabbed my gun.

"Where are we going?" Chase said, pushing his gun and blade in his back.

"Chase, Cam and I have got this. Just stay with the girls please," I asked him.

I needed someone here with Honey, flip mode and the thugettes, and my kids.

"I got you," Chase said and dapped me up.

I looked at Cam and he nodded his head at me. We walked out the house and climbed in my car.

"Let's go get my brother," he said and we dapped.

All I could do was pray I was right as I drove to an area I hadn't been to in years. Papa De didn't want to sell or rent his home as it held memories of Delano and Miss Brenda. He brought a few of their favorite personal items with him to his island but for the most part, the house was untouched.

I turned off my headlights as we entered the compound. The barn was in the far back a little up from the house, so I headed there. We used it to cook up our food and also it was where I did most of my training with Papa De and Unc. Once we had my city on lock, we moved everything into the town but the barn was still standing.

My heart raced as I stopped the car outside the barn. I turned my phone on silent and looked over at Cam.

"We ready?" I asked and he nodded. I knew all this shit was new to Cam, he wasn't from these streets like me and the boys. I took my gun from my waist and slipped out the car. I told Cam to go in the front and I went around the back.

250

I forced the side door open and crept in. My hunch was right, as there was a light on inside so clearly somebody was inside.

I looked around and above me to make sure no one was around. I crept to the door where the light was coming from and Cam came in towards me. I nodded my head and held up three fingers.

I dropped one to signal I was counting and when I dropped the other, I kicked the door and raised my gun.

And there was Ricky, tied to a chair in the middle of the room, surrounded by three men. I shot and killed one as Cameron shot the other. The third took off running through another door and Cameron chased after him. I pushed my gun in my back and dashed to Ricky.

"Ricky. Ricky," I said, shaking him but he was out cold. I heard footsteps and I assumed it was Cameron until I looked up – and found the snake.

"What the fuck!"

Chapter Seventeen

Honey

I was nervous when Ky-mani left out the house with Cameron. I hoped that they did find Ricky but I hoped they weren't walking into a place full of men because there was only two of them.

My stomach felt sick as anxiety ate away at it. Tasha and the girls tried to calm me down but I just couldn't shake a feeling that something just wasn't right.

I jumped up to go speak to Chase. But when I approached Ky-mani's office to talk to him, I heard him on the phone talking about Monae. I can't believe I forgot about that bitch!

When he turned to face me, I folded my arms across my chest. "What up, sis?" he smiled but I wasn't smiling with him.

"Take me to Monae," I said.

"Honey, you know I can't do that. Law said

252

you were to stay here."

"Chase! That bitch sent men into the house to kill me, she arranged for another nigga to come into my home as I slept to rape and kill me. I want to know why; I have the right to know why. Ky-mani will just kill her and I will never know why she did it because he won't tell me even if he knew. So, I'm asking you as my brother to take me to her."

"Either that or I'm going to run out of here and you will have to explain to Ky-mani why I was outside alone. All you have to do is take me and we can avoid that," I smiled at him.

"Chase, you better or no pussy for you," Tasha came up and said causing us to laugh. This bitch was fronting because Chase could hold off from sex a lot longer than she could.

"Honey, I swear your ass isn't right," he shook his head at me.
"I don't want to take you but I believe your crazy ass will run up outta here anyway, so I would rather you went with me," he huffed and headed for the door.

253

"Sydney, watch the kids, please. We will be back soon," I said to her and grabbed my purse.

"How did you know I was coming too?" Tasha asked and I laughed.

"Bitch, your ass is nosey. I knew you would want to come," I said and she laughed.

We jumped in Chase's car and headed to the pier.

We climbed out and followed him into a warehouse door. He led us into the back through another door and then I saw her. She was chained up and inside a cage that was hanging from the ceiling. Tasha and I chuckled as we looked at that pitiful bitch.

"Well, well, well," I sang and she looked at me.

"Where is Ky-mani, bitch?" she spat at me. I looked at Chase's niggas who were watching her when I came in.

Chase nodded and they lowered the cage to the floor. I walked over to it and kicked it making Monae shake.

"Now, now Monae what have I told you about name calling? My name is Honey Unique Parker. Say it after me," I taunted her like she was a little one- year-old learning how to talk.

"What the fuck you mean Parker?" she asked.

"Oh, I'm sorry. Look," I said, lifting my left hand showing my wedding band. Her eyes popped out of her head.

"I should thank you, though. Because after your little stunt in Miami, Ky-mani didn't want to wait anymore to get married," I smiled, took my cell out and showed her a photo that I took with Ky-mani on my wedding day.

"WHY WON'T YOU JUST DIE, BITCH!!!" she roared as tears slid down her face.

"Why are you trying so hard to get rid of me, Monae? I never did anything to you!" I yelled back.

"Yes, you did! You stole my man and my life. I'm the only bitch supposed to be with Ky-mani and have his kids."

"You mean the same kids you inseminated yourself with Ky-mani's seeds to get?" I asked and her jaw dropped open.

"Yeah we know all about that. Ky-mani had someone go to your house and they found your stash in the freezer," I informed her.

"Nasty, bitch! Most people have frozen veg, ice cream, and shit in theirs but you got motherfucking babies on ice!" Tasha spat laughing.

"You may want to lie to me, Monae, but stop lying to your damn self. Wake up and open your eyes. You really believe killing me would make Ky-mani want you?" I asked and this delusional bitch said yes.

"Come on, Monae! Even if I did die, he still wouldn't have wanted you. You've known him for nine years and you believe that if he hadn't wifed you in all that time - he was going to now? When was the last time you even fucked him Monae? Mani is four years old and I know you haven't slept with Ky-mani since you got pregnant. That shit had nothing to do with me! I wasn't even in the picture then. He was fucking Angel and other bitches. I ain't the problem, you are. Because you're too got damn stupid to see that Ky-mani just doesn't want you!"

"You think I care about that shit? He may not have wanted me and that's fine. I just didn't want him with you! I could care less about Angel and all them other bitches because he didn't love them but HE LOVED YOU!"

256

"So for that, I needed to die?" I asked.

"Yes, bitch! If I can't have Ky-mani then you sure couldn't!" I looked in her eyes and saw a lost woman.

"You know Ky-mani wants to kill you but I told him not to. I want you to live every day knowing that you failed in your attempts to get my husband," I turned to walk away but she started laughing.

"You think you're so perfect but your life is fucked up and you don't even know it. You think you've won? All I wanted was you dead and gone but I guess Ky-mani will die instead. And then you will have to live with the fact that it was your own brother the whole time! Imagine that – your own family killed your husband," she laughed and my eyes bucked out of my head.

"What did you just say?!"

"Cameron. He's The Don, bitch," she laughed uncontrollably.

I looked back at Chase and all the color had left his face. Ky-mani was alone somewhere with Cameron!

"Enjoy being a single mother and widow, bitch!

Y'all might as well kill me so that I can be in paradise with my baby daddy," she laughed.

Tasha took off running and delivered a kick through the bars and knocked Monae so hard, her front teeth fell out. "Talk too much, bitch!" Tasha spat.

My hands started to shake and sweat. I had no idea where Ky-mani was or if he was even still alive. Tears flooded my face as I ran out of the warehouse to Chase's car. I unlocked it and jumped right in. Thank God he had handed me the keys to hold because he had no pockets on the shorts he was wearing. Chase and Tasha ran out after me but I took off speeding out of the grounds.

"Ky-mani, where are you?" I asked no one in particular as his phone kept ringing out and going to voicemail. Suddenly, I remembered that we linked our phones together so if anything happened, he could find me. I activated my phone locator app and it showed me where he was.

"Please, Lord," I prayed as I sped to save my husband.

Law

"Cameron, what the fuck you doing, man? You were the snake this whole time?" I asked.

"No," he said, sending a shot to my shoulder, the impact made me fall back onto the floor. I looked up and Ricky was still out cold.

"I wasn't the snake, Ky-mani; I'm The Don," he smiled crazily at me.

"I had Joe pretend to be me but it was me the whole time. I sent those young niggas to try to kidnap you..."

"And rape your sister!" I yelled.

"She's no longer my sister! You infected her with your filth. I was trying to get her away from you when I told Trixie to burn her house down. I was hoping she would think being with you was trouble but she held on. She's so in love with you that I know she would never side with me now."

"Why, Cameron?" I heard a voice asking and I looked up to see my Unc standing in the doorway.

"Pop? What are you doing here?" Cameron asked, picking up one of my guns off the floor and aiming it at my Unc with the other still on me.

"I realized it was you son," he said lowly.

"How?" Cameron asked.

"I didn't until you called me earlier and said that when this was all over, we could buy a family home and live happily, but it was when you said a bigger house than the Miami one, that I knew. How would you have known how big it was unless you were there? I knew you hadn't supposedly arrived in Miami and that you weren't due to come until the day after the attack on us," my Unc said.

"How could you come into my house with those men, knowing our family was there Cameron?" I asked.

"YOUR FAMILY, Ky-mani, not mine! You took my Pop and my only sister away from me!" he yelled. "And you, Pop. How could you hand over everything to Ky-mani? He ain't your son! This empire should have been mine. I should have been the King of these Streets not him."

"Cam, I tried to bring you along with me but your interest was pussy, my nigga, not the streets or money," I said.

"Nigga, fuck you, you wanted me to be your got damn partner or deputy and I wanted it all to myself."

"Cameron you couldn't have handled a responsibility like that! I made a decision and I'm not

260

sorry about that. If Papa De and I handed it over to you, that empire would have died out a long time ago. You wouldn't have had a clue what to do," my Unc said.

"You could have shown me!"

"Cameron, I did! I tried many times to get you in and teach you but whenever we held meetings your ass was in some pussy somewhere. You think I was going to wait around? I wanted to retire and hand my place down and you weren't interested!"

"So you handed it all to this nigga from the fucking ghetto with his poor ass. The fatherless bastard," he said and I jumped to my feet.

"Nigga, fuck you! Don't ever talk about my Pops being dead. You ain't no fucking man, Cameron. You couldn't walk a motherfucking day in my shoe, nigga. You thought you could take me out but I'm still here, nigga!" I growled.

"Yeah but for how long, Cuz? I doubt even you could walk off a bullet to the head – ask KY," he laughed, pushing his gun to my forehead.

"Cameron, no please!" I heard Honey's voice ring out in the barn.

"Ayo, sis, welcome to the party. I'm glad you're here, now you can watch me kill your husband. And then I'm gonna kill his momma, his sisters, and his kids. You know I never thought of doing all of this shit until Monae whispered in my ear and sat on my dick. Man, that hoe gave me all that I needed trying to get rid of Honey. Nigga, didn't I tell you about fucking that hoe?" Cameron laughed.

"Whoa, sis – back the fuck up. Don't come near me, I know Law taught your ass how to shoot," he chuckled.

He pressed the gun into my head and I turned slightly so I could see Honey. She stood there trembling with fear and her face was full of tears. I smiled at her trying to calm her down. Cameron wiggled the gun to get my attention and I turned back to face him.

"Let's play a little game, Law. Before I kill you, I want you to choose who dies first out of your loved ones. Would it be A, my Pop; your uncle. B, your cousin or C, your pregnant wife? One of them is going to die before you but I want you to pick," he chuckled at me.

With one gun still pressed into my head, he

swung the other gun between the other three.

But then he stopped the gun on Honey.

"Cameron, don't!" my Unc said.

"Pop, move," Cameron said and I knew at that point that Unc had stepped in front of her. He pushed the gun into my head and forced me back towards them. I looked to see my Unc with arms out blocking Honey.

"I want Law to see his wife die and know how it feels to see his family taken from him, the way I had to when my own family loved him more than me. Y'all are my family but your loyalty is to him," he snarled.

I thought about going for the gun he had pointed at towards Honey and Unc but I knew he would easily shoot me or them before I could pull the trigger on him myself. I knew at that point that we weren't all walking out here alive!

Suddenly, Honey lunged towards him and stabbed a pen into his shoulder.

"Arrghh, you bitch!" he spat and raised his gun at her.

263

"Noooo!" I yelled and grabbed his hand.

POP!

I heard and then the sound of Cameron's body hitting the floor. I looked around and Ricky was holding my gun that I put down by his feet when Cameron forced me to disarm myself.

"Crazy, motherfucker," he said weakly before cracking a smile. I grabbed Honey into my arms and kissed her before dashing over to Ricky.

"My nigga, you good?" I asked my cousin and he nodded.

Unc came over to help me pick up Ricky after putting another shot into Cameron's leaking head.

"What? I needed to make sure he was dead. He turned on his family for greed, that shit is unforgivable, son or not," he said when we all looked at him.

We carried Ricky to my car and put him in. I called Turbo and told him to get the clean-up crew before taking Ricky to the hospital.

"Shit, I forgot about Monae," I hugged Honey as we sat in the waiting room as Ricky was seen to.

"I called my cousin; his friends at the women's jail are about to have another tenant." Honey laughed.

I would much rather have Monae killed but Honey didn't want that. No matter how she got them, she was still the kids' mother. So I would allow her ONE pass if she stayed gone!

A few hours later and Ricky was released, he was suffering my dehydration but he was good.

Finally, we were all together, safe and happy.

SIP KY. We got him for you. I prayed for my fallen soldier.

"Ayo, Turbo, do me a favor, nigga," I whispered to him as we walked into the house.

"Anything, Law."

"Find Trixie and make her disappear," I said and he smiled.

"On it."

What? She burnt down Honey's crib; she

265

couldn't be pardoned for that!

I did say I was gonna find the person who took my baby's smile away and what I say I do!

After all, they call me Law!

Ha!

<u>Chapter Eighteen</u>

Honey

One year later

Ky-mani and I had a new baby girl called Kylani. She looked like him but had my eyes.

Our little family was complete and we were happy. She was a thriving fifteen weeks old.

Drake and Kelis had a boy named Drake Junior; he was Drake's twin, all Kelis did was carry him. And guess what, the bitch was pregnant again already! I think somebody needs to buy a got damn TV!

Today was our family wedding day. Ky-mani made it a big, all-expenses paid event. He invited all of our family, including my momma and Gran, as well as half the town. We hired the huge church in town and the reception was being held on a private gated ground. The news channel was there too; it was a huge affair!

The girls and Ky-mani's sisters were my
bridesmaids. I chose a coral dress for them this time
that was long and strapless with diamonds and roses
on one side.

Their hair was styled in a curly updo with
diamond studded Bobby pins and diamond tiaras.
They wore pearl earrings, necklace, and
bracelet. They each held a bouquet of white lilies
held together with a coral ribbon.

For me, I had a Hayley Paige, Gracie strapless
fit-to-flare silk organza embroidered dress with
scattered flowered motifs and heart cut out back.
My hair was in a braided pin up with a long
four foot back veil and a diamond encrusted mini
crown. My makeup was nude with coral smoky eye
and coral blush. I had diamond leave shaped earrings
and matching necklace.
My bouquet was white roses and diamanté pins,
tied together with a huge coral bow. Mani and Chyna
wore white and coral too.

All my groomsmen had white suits with a
coral waistcoat and tie and white shoes.

My girls and I rode to the church in an all-white limousine with coral ribbons on the front. My momma and Gran rode in the limo too with Marco and the kids. Aunt Ruth and Momma Doreen rode with Ky-mani and the groomsmen.

The church was full to capacity and bursting at the seams. The news crews were all posted outside and when I stepped out of the limo, the lights of camera flashing came from all around. I posed on the white carpet for some pictures with my girls, until the wedding planner said it was time to go in. Each one of my girls paired up with their men, and Toya walked with Troy as Nevaeh walked with TJ.

The bridal party walked down to Whitney Houston's "I Believe In You and Me."

"You look so beautiful, baby," Marco whispered to me and kissed my cheek.

"Thank you, Daddy," I said and he looked at me with tears in his eyes. It took me a while but he was my dad and I loved him.

The doors to the church opened for me to descend down to Ky-mani and everybody stood to their feet.

The soulful sound of Jennifer Hudson "I'm

Giving Myself" began to play and I stepped out.

I saw Ky-mani standing at the alter in a crisp all white suit and coral waistcoat and flower on the outside. His dreads were so neat and braided down his back. He looked at me and we locked eyes. He smiled as I walked down to him. I looked over at my momma and she was crying bucket loads and so were my girls.

I dropped my eyes back to Ky-mani and a huge smile washed over my face. I got to marry my best friend again!

Kylani made a little sound sitting in my gran's lap and I smiled at her. She was the perfect product of me and the love of my life.

When I finally made it to Ky-mani, he grabbed me and kissed me so deeply and passionately I couldn't help but shed a few tears.

We had been through so much in almost two years but it brought us here to this perfect moment. When we broke our kiss, everyone cheered and clapped. I laughed and he wiped my tears away.

He turned to my dad and they hugged each other. "Dearly beloved, we are gathered here for the reunion of these two people in love. God has been good to them and made it possible for us to share in this joyous day with them. They married before but they wanted to re-proclaim their love for each other in front of all their loved ones. Ky-mani, you may speak first," the Pastor said.

"Honey, where do I start, baby? I know God truly loves me because he took time out to make you just for me. I would marry you a thousand times over! You are my air, Honey, my heart beat, my very existence and I promise baby to love you for the rest of my life and beyond. Thank you for loving me too, baby," he said and rubbed my cheek. *I love you.* He mouthed and I smiled.

"Ky-mani, you're proof that there is a God because He brought you to me. I love you with my whole being, past my soul, Ky-mani. As the song said, I'm giving myself to you. Every day I wake up thankful to having you here with me.

My life has no meaning without you and I don't want to ever know how that feels. We are connected for life, baby," I said and he laughed.

I turned to Mani and Chyna, Ky-mani handed me

271

two little rings that I got for them.

"Mani, Chyna, this ring is my promise to you both," I said, slipping it on their little fingers.

"I promise to love, cherish and protect you. I promise to be the best woman, momma, friend and provider as long as I live," I said and kissed them both on the cheeks.

The Pastor bound mine and Ky-mani's hands together in a white ribbon.

"What God hath joined together, let not man put asunder," the pastor said. "It's my great pleasure to pronounce you man and wife again. You may kiss your bride again, Ky-mani," he smiled.

With a big smile on his face, Ky-mani pulled me in close and we sealed our love with a romantic kiss. I closed my eyes and my mind brought me back to that day when I first saw him in my office and then the day I sat with him at the park.

Those days led me to here and I couldn't be happier!

The room erupted into the loudest cheer I had ever heard. Ky-mani wrapped me in his arms and kissed the top of my head. My Gran handed me Kylani and we walked out with our children.

I looked at my family; my husband and kids, as we rode to the reception. I thanked God for them and prayed over them.

We ate and partied down. I danced away with my girls and every once in a while, I looked up to see Ky-mani looking at me smiling. With Kylani in his hands, he walked over to me.

"Hey, Mrs. Parker," he winked.

"Hey, Mr. Parker," I smiled and kissed him.

"Ahem," we heard and turned to see my momma looking at us.

"Ky-mani, didn't I tell you not to give Honey any babies before I met you?" she said putting her hands on her hips.

"Ma, it wasn't my fault. I went to bed and woke up, then Honey was pregnant. I didn't even do anything," he said and we laughed.

"Boy, you just lucky you made an honest woman out of her," she said.

"Ma, trust me. She was an honest woman long

273

before that," he winked at me.

"And that's why I love you, baby," my momma said, squeezing his cheeks.

"May I have this dance?" my dad came over and asked.

"Sure, Pops," I smiled and took his hand.

"I can't believe life brought us together Honey. I thought that I would never see you again," he said with his voice shaking.

"I guess we were both supposed to meet, Ky-mani," I smiled.

"Yeah. When I met this cocky 17-year-old, who would have known that he would lead me to my baby," he said, kissing my cheek.

I stared into his eyes and I saw both joy and sadness. And I knew it was because of Cameron. It's sad that things turned out the way it did and sometimes I wish things could have been different but Cameron chose his path.

I danced for a few more songs with my dad before taking a seat for a little breather. TJ came and sat down next to me.

"What's up, Cuz?" he said and I nodded.

"Sorry to rain on your day but I just wanted you to know another hit," he said.

I looked at him for a few seconds before shaking my head.

"Thanks, TJ, I couldn't think of a better present," I smiled and winked at him.

I got up and went over to Ky-mani. I pulled on his arm and hugged my arms around his neck.

"Another hit, baby, can you believe it?" I said to him and he shook his head, as he swayed our bodies to the beat of the music.

"So what you gone do?"

"I think it's time now. Enough is enough," I said and he nodded.

"Do your thing, baby," he said before spinning me and dipping me to the music.

"I love you so much," he said, kissing my lips.

"I love you more."

Monae

Earlier that day

I couldn't believe my eyes when I saw the news reporting about Ky-mani's and Honey's wedding day! I was sat here rotting away in this jail that Ky- mani's bitch put me in and he was out there celebrating and showing the world he was marrying that bitch again!

Ooohhh I hated that bitch!!!!

I got 25 years because of her for killing Pete. Look I had to. The second that nigga pushed his tongue into my mouth, I already knew what he was after. And for two weeks straight I had to fuck this nigga until something in me snapped.

I stabbed him and slit his throat as he slept in bed. A part of me did it thinking it was Honey's pretty ass but mainly it was because I was mad that after all my planning to get Law, I ended up right back with Pete!

I looked back up at the TV and scoffed. The camera showed Ky-mani holding his new baby. She was so cute and looked just like him. I couldn't contain the jealousy that I felt. I wanted to bust the

276

TV monitor but weren't anybody trying to spend time in solitary.

I had to do something. I couldn't just let them have a happily ever after. Yeah, I know I must be crazy to still be caught up on him but y'all, believe me, weren't anybody like him!

In a rage, I stormed back to my cell.

"What's wrong with you?" my fine ass guard said. He was a new transfer and had been in my jail for six months and in those six months, I was able to get whatever I wanted from him. But I never ever asked for what I really wanted – until now!

I pushed him up against my wall, yanked down his pants, and started giving him the best sloppy head ever. I sucked his dick like my life depended on it.

"Ahh, shit Monae. You better stop before I nut. I want some of that pussy first."

Yeah – I was fucking him. Hey, don't hate me! Never underestimate the power of pussy!

I quickly jumped up, pulled my jail pants down and bent over. He slipped on a condom and slid up into my wetness.

"Ahhh," he grunted behind me.

"So, Teegan, I need a favor, baby," I said in my sweetest, most seductive voice I could muster up.

"Shit! Monae, anything for you," he grunted and pounded away into me.

"My ex-best friend who set me up and put me in here, she keeps taunting me about what she did in letters. But she went a step too far and married my boyfriend. I want her to pay and suffer for what she's done. Even us she's affecting. If I wasn't in here, we could have been happy and together," I said, making sure to throw it all the way back on him as he liked.

"Oohhhh, baby," he shuddered and curled his feet in his shoes.

"Please, baby – would you do it if I let you fuck me in my ass like you've been wanting to?" I begged.

The whole six months we had been messing around, he had asked me if he could and I told him hell no, but I was ready to give in if it meant Honey would finally die!

"Monae, I will kill anybody if you let me do that," he said smiling.

He wet his dick up nicely with some spit and then eased his way into my asshole.

"Got damn it!" he moaned out as he stretched my ass. I clenched my teeth and took this hit for the purpose.

Afterward, we sat adjusting our clothes.

"So what's her name?" he asked and I smiled widely.

****

A week later and my ass finally healed. I hadn't seen Teegan since I asked him to kill Honey. I just hoped he succeeded.

I sat in my cell wondering how he killed the bitch; did he shoot her, stab her, slice her throat and let her bleed to death? The thought was so sweet, it made my pussy drip.

"Monae, you have a special visitation today, so we've brought your lunch to you and then you are to go right on down," Teegan said, walking in and handing me a tray of food. I smiled knowing that it was Ky-mani, I had been sending him letters to visit me; I guess he finally did!

"Teegan, did you do it?" I whispered as I tucked into my meal. I needed to know when I saw Ky-mani that he was now single. And with me in here, he would never suspect me.

"Yes, it was taken care of," he said, handing me a Polaroid picture. I looked at it, and it was of Ky-mani dressed in black at the graveside with the kids and baby. I couldn't help the smile that formed on my face. Finally, that bitch was dead and I won!

"When was this taken?" I asked with a mouth full of Mac and cheese. I don't know if it was because I knew Honey was finally gone but this food tasted so good.
"Early yesterday morning. They had a small private service," Teegan said.

"Well, Monae, this is goodbye; I'm getting transferred back. I know I will never see you again," he smiled.
Something about his smile made me feel uneasy

but my mind was occupied with Ky-mani; plus, I didn't have to fuck Teegan anymore, so I was glad he was going.

"Thank you for everything but before you go, do you know who's here to visit me?"

"Um, someone by the surname of Parker. That's all I was told. See you, Monae." And he left my cell.

Ky-mani had finally come to his senses and came to me. I'm glad he picked the special visit, they allowed sexual activities to happen and I definitely was trying to comfort him with my pussy, that's for sure!

I finished off my meal and headed to the bathroom to brush my teeth and freshen up. Then I headed down to see my baby daddy.

I walked into the room and he wasn't there yet, so I took a seat at the table and waited. When I heard the door open, I planted a huge smile on my face and turned to face it.

What the fuck!

"Surprised to see me?" Honey asked me,

281

walking in and taking a seat at the desk. She crossed her legs and placed her hands on her knee. "Huh?" she said.

I looked behind me to see if Ky-mani would come in but he never did.

"Where's, Ky-mani?" I asked. She smiled and then reached across the table and slapped the slob from my mouth.

"Ow," I said and then I tasted blood in my mouth.

"Didn't I tell you not to speak my husband's name again, bitch?! I warned you, I told you to stay the fuck away from him and my kids. What you thought my ass was playing? Well, you had your chance, Monae. I just came so you could see my face one last time. I told I would kill you, didn't I?" she smirked.

"Yeah and how you plan on doing that with me in here, Honey?" I smiled.

She stood to her feet with her eyes trained on me. "I already killed you, bitch," she spat.

And with that, she walked towards the door but then stopped before opening it.

"Oh yeah, here," she said, coming back to

place something down on the table before leaving.

I stared at the door for a while to make sure she was gone before I turned my attention to the pamphlet she had placed down. It was showing the back, so I turned it over and damn near had a heart attack.

It was the funeral handout – with my face on it! And the date of death was today!!!

I walked back to my cell twitching at every sight and sound. I was so afraid that I didn't even leave my cell for supper. I kept imagining someone stabbing me with a dirty homemade shank.

But as the hours passed, I slowly started feeling reassured that she just gave me an empty threat hoping to scare me off. But now I knew she was all bark but no bite, I was definitely far fromdone.

"This bitch really had me shook and paranoid for nothing," I sucked my teeth and chuckled. I coughed as something tickled my throat. I was so mad at Teegan, he told me it was done!

His ass is so lucky he transferred, I sucked my teeth. But when I did, I tasted the unexpected taste of blood in my mouth. I knew my mouth bled a little after Honey slapped me but that was hours ago and it stopped.

I started coughing again and this time I tasted more blood. I ran my fingers in my mouth and when I pulled them out, they were covered in blood.

"Oh my God," I said when reality finally hit me – Honey killed me. But how, other than a slap she did nothing.

Then my eyes fell to the tray I still had from the food I ate earlier and my blood ran cold.

"HELP ME!!!" I screamed and banged on the door. "Please!! Somebody help," I continued to bang on the door. I felt my chest tighten and I panicked.

"Ok, Richards, what's all the noise about?" A fat, short, fair skinned warden asked me.

"I need urgent medical attention. I've been poisoned by my baby father's wife. She wants me dead."

"Yeah? And how would she have done that with you behind bars?" she asked, dropping her hands onto her hips.

"She was here today! She poisoned me. Look, I'm bleeding from my mouth."

She stood there and casually flicked through the pages on a clipboard that she was holding.

"Says here that you never had any visitors today or any other day in fact," she told me.

"Please, she was here."

"It just looks like you've busted the inside of your mouth on something. Pipe down inmate; I'm not in the mood for your foolishness tonight. Go rinse out your mouth with water and lay down. One more peep out of you and it's the hole for you," she growled before slamming and locking the door behind her.

I ran over to the little metal sink that was in a corner and began to rinse my mouth out. I started coughing uncontrollably and spat up blood. I dropped to my knees and clenched my chest as my wind pipes closed up and I starved of oxygen.

I fall flat on my face and with my last breath, I breathed out –

"I hate that, bitch!"

Honey

I know what you must be thinking, did sweet old Honey really poison and kill Monae? I sure did. I warned her and tried to give her the chance but she just wouldn't let go. Ky-mani wanted her dead months ago but it was me who had him spare her and for what? This bitch was still at my head so she had to go.

Teegan worked over at TJ's jail house. He had him transferred to see if Monae had something planned for me and she sure did. On my wedding day, TJ told me that she ordered Teegan to take me out.

I spoke to Ky-mani and he told me to go ahead. I felt bad looking at the kids knowing I would have to kill their momma but she abandoned and stopped being their mother a long time ago.

In all the letters she wrote to Ky-mani she never asked about them and if I'm honest, they were the only reason why I didn't kill her before.

It took a week but I finally put my plan in motion. TJ organized to have the security cameras turned off during my visit; all the staff was told to ignore Monae regarding her being poisoned and the governor, Eric, had her food poisoned for me. The obituary, I did just to strike fear into her.

The photo of Ky-mani was of him visiting KY. We finally had a private service for him. We never recovered his body but he deserved a burial.

I strutted to my own beat when I got back home to my husband.

We had been through hell and back but finally we had peace and my little headache, Monae, was finally gone.

What?

Just call me Mrs. Ky-mani LAW Parker!!!

Ooowww!!!

The End

56613723R00178

Made in the USA
San Bernardino, CA
13 November 2017